bye for now

A Wishers Story

Wish big!

Kathleen Chodzan

bye for now
A Wishers Story

Kathleen Churchyard

EGMONT
USA
New York

EGMONT

We bring stories to life

First published by Egmont USA, 2011
443 Park Avenue South, Suite 806
New York, NY 10016

1 3 5 7 9 8 6 4 2

www.egmontusa.com
KathleenChurchyard.com

Library of Congress Cataloging-in-Publication Data
Churchyard, Kathleen.
Bye for now : a Wishers story / Kathleen Churchyard.
p. cm.
Summary: While blowing out the candles on her birthday cake,
eleven-year-old Robin wishes she were someone else, and wakes up
to find herself in the body of an eleven-year-old British actress.
ISBN 978-1-60684-190-7 (hardcover) — ISBN 978-1-60684-278-2 (electronic
book) [1. Wishes—Fiction. 2. London (England)—Fiction. 3. England—Fiction.]
I. Title.
PZ7.C476By 2011
[Fic]—dc22
2011005895

Printed in the United States of America

CPSIA tracking label information:
Printed in July 2011 at Berryville Graphics, Berryville, Virginia

To the wishers who inspired this book
—my daughters Emma and Rowan.
And in fond memory of their friend,
Rachael Albertson.

ACKNOWLEDGMENTS

In true British tradition, I'd like to say "cheers" to my husband, Paul, for encouraging me to write; to friend Melissa Kennedy, for her prompt editorial notes; to my agent, Faye Bender, for her relentless faith in this book; to my editor, Ruth Katcher; and to the staff at Egmont, for making my dream a reality. And a very special thanks to my wonderful, wonderful little editors-in-training: Chandler Lawing, Merrill Douglass, Hannah Patrum, Alexis Black, Delaney and Maya Kelnhofer, Gabrielle Beaudry, Anissa Thaddeus, Pamela Beane-Fox, Madison Hobbs, Riley Olson, Samantha Badgett.

chapter one

Robin Haggersly of Concord, North Carolina, makes a wish

THE HORRIBLE BIRTHDAY BEGAN WITH A black eye.

SMACK. Dizziness. Pain. Through her other eye, Robin looked to see what she'd hit—a head of white-blonde hair—Sophie.

"Ow. OW. OWWW!" Robin giggled nervously as she covered her eye with both hands to smush the pain. "I'M OKAY!" she shouted to anyone who might be listening. She was so dizzy she wobbled. "Soph, you all right?"

Eight-year-old Sophie was silent, one hand feeling all over her head for damage. Uh-oh. Tears were only seconds away. Robin wrapped a consoling arm around her sister, keeping her other hand in place over her eye. "C'mon, let's go and see Mom." They staggered into their parents' room. "MOM! WE BONKED HEADS!" Robin giggled again while Sophie let out a sob and rushed to their mom's arms. Typical. Sophie was going to cry, and Robin was going to get in trouble.

"What happened?" her mom demanded, pulling Sophie into a cuddle.

"Robin HURT ME!" Sophie wailed. "She did it on purpose!"

"Did NOT!" Robin argued, but she was still laughing. Never a good thing to do.

"Okay, okay." Her mom turned to Robin. "Your sister appears to be hurt. Do you think you could stop laughing for just a minute, please?"

The note of impatience in her mom's voice sucked the laughter right out of Robin. She pulled her hand away from her eye and placed it on her hip in self-defense. She was tired of Sophie always getting her in trouble. And today was HER birthday!

The gesture was all Robin needed. Her mom took one look at her eye and said, "Oh, honey." She turned to Sophie. "Get your sister some ice, quick. How do you feel?" Robin felt a momentary surge of triumph over her little sister, but her satisfaction disappeared a moment later when her mom peered into her face and said, "It's swelling like mad.... Maybe I should call Dr. Douglass."

Robin's stomach flip-flopped with fresh worry as she looked into the mirror. Her entire left eye was blackening, along with part of her cheek. Her face looked scary, but NO WAY was she missing the conference swim meet or her birthday sleepover, just to end up at the doctor's office. The day—*her day*—was on the line. She turned to her mom, curled her hands into fists, and smiled until she felt her cheeks pressing against the wound. "You shoulda seen the other guy."

Her mom laughed as a worried Sophie silently handed her a plastic bag filled with ice. Mom pressed it to Robin's eye and ordered, "Keep that on your eye while you get your swimsuit."

Relieved, Robin tried to recollect what had happened while she dug out her swimsuit, swim cap, and goggles. Mom had woken her up by crooning, "Happy Birthday," and telling her they had to be at the conference by 8:00. Their chocolate Lab, Kitty, had jumped on the bed and licked Robin's face. She'd been so excited that her feet had skittered across the wooden floors, and energy had seemed to radiate from her fingertips. It was her birthday! And the conference swim meet! Plus, presents, dinner, and a sleepover with her BFF! Excited, Robin had whipped open the bathroom door ... and then she'd run into Sophie.

Robin examined the wound again in the mirror as she tugged on her suit. It's just a black eye, she insisted to herself. Big deal. Nothing was going to ruin today. She snapped the shoulders of her black-and-red Breakers suit to emphasize her point and headed downstairs, only to turn around. She'd forgotten the ice pack.

In the kitchen, Aaron dumped a package with a Florida address in front of Robin. "Happy birthday.

Looks like your gift from Grandma. What'd ya do to your eye?"

Robin ignored the question as she scarfed down her bagel. She groaned inwardly as Alia walked in behind her brother. Were they giving Aaron's spacy girlfriend a ride to the meet again? Since Alia came along, Aaron didn't talk to Robin much, and she missed him. He was pretty cool for an older brother. At fourteen, he was funny and smart, even if he was occasionally obnoxious. He was also incredibly popular, which wouldn't hurt Robin's social status when she started at Concord Middle School this fall. Aaron could have had any girl he wanted—so why had he picked Alia? Sure, she was pretty, but everybody knew she was weird. She'd made herself famous at school last year by cutting off all her hair in the parking lot in front of her mom. Word had it she kept screaming, "You don't know me!" while she was doing it. The whole school thought she was nuts. Aaron apparently found it irresistible.

Robin eyed the package. Grandma always sent a doll, from wherever she and her new husband were traveling in the world. The card was brief. "Have a wonderful birthday. Eleven is a magical number." Robin tossed the card aside and ripped open the box.

"A doll." Robin's voice was flat as she planted it unceremoniously on the table. Not even a good doll, one she could still play with when nobody was looking.

4

It was weird, actually—no arms or legs, just a solid wooden body painted in multiple colors.

Aaron looked at it and teased, "Aww, it's a dolly for sissy!"

"Stop it, Aaron!" Robin responded automatically, but she felt a flush of embarrassment rushing to her face. It was bad enough she got a doll for her birthday. Now he had to make fun of her, too? In front of Alia?

Aaron scooped up the doll and cradled it. "But it's so cute! What're you going to name it?" Lifting it to his ear he said, "What's that? You want your mommy? Okay—"

Robin swatted at him, but he just laughed. She jumped and tried to grab the doll back, but he held it high, well out of her reach. Sometimes she really hated being short.

Alia plucked the doll out of Aaron's hand from behind and muttered, "Aaron, c'mon." She looked at the doll wistfully before handing it back to Robin.

"What is it?" Sophie asked, scrunching her nose.

Alia answered, "It's a *matryoshka*. It's Russian. There are more dolls inside. Twist at the middle, Robin," she instructed. Robin did and the doll split in two. Inside she found a smaller version of the same doll. Hearing a rattle, she twisted again. Another one. Despite her disinterest, Robin kept going until she'd opened nine dolls, while Sophie lined them up neatly in a long, descending row.

Alia picked up the biggest doll and pointed to a picture painted in an oval on the doll's chest. "Every *matryoshka* tells a fairy tale. This one's the story of the firebird. A king orders his prince to catch the firebird, because it keeps stealing apples from his tree." Picking up the next doll, she pointed again to the delicate, hand-painted picture on the doll's tummy. "The prince steals the bird, but he can't resist stealing her golden cage, too." Alia reached for the third doll. "The king who owns the bird catches him. This king declares that if the prince wants his freedom, he must steal the magical white horse that belongs to yet another king in a neighboring province. The prince tries, but he's caught again." Alia picked up doll number four. "This king demands the prince steal a beautiful princess. So he does, but he falls in love with her himself."

Robin examined the picture on the fifth doll. The radiantly orange firebird was in mid-flight, illuminating a path in the darkness for the prince and princess who rode together on the white steed. The princess's features were daintily painted. She wore a demure smile on her face, and her flowing blonde hair waved in the wind.

Alia's voice grew soft as she looked at doll number six. "The prince decides he's going to keep everything he's stolen. BUT"—she picked up the tiny seventh doll—"when he returns home, his brothers see his amazing stuff and are so jealous they try to kill him."

Alia held the last two tiny dolls, one in each hand. "A magical wolf kills them, the prince marries the princess, and they live happily ever after."

"So, it's a fable about coveting," said Aaron.

Robin was still irritated with her brother, but she really liked Alia's story. She couldn't resist asking, "What's coveting?"

"Wanting something that belongs to someone else," her brother explained. "The moral of the story is while you're eyeing someone else's stuff, somebody's eyeing yours."

Alia nodded. "You don't get what you want without sacrifice."

Robin was lost, although she guessed they were talking about something other than the doll. She turned to Alia. "How do you KNOW all this Russian stuff?"

Alia shrugged. "I don't know. I just do."

Robin's mom clapped her hands in the doorway. "Registration is in thirty minutes. Alia, I promised your mom we'd be on time. Everybody in the van!!!" She picked up the smallest *matryoshka*. "Isn't this cute!"

Although it was only 7:30, the air was already thick and soupy with July heat. Summer in the South. Robin had often wished her birthday were at some other time of year—winter, spring, fall—all of which were nice in North Carolina. But in July, the temperature often hit one hundred degrees.

7

In the van, Robin's ice pack dripped on her leg, a constant reminder of both the heat and her wound. She tried to focus on the swim meet. Truth was, she hated swim team. And she especially hated conference. Hated it. But the athletic Haggersly parents had only surrendered to Aaron's and Robin's begging to join Eastcliff Swim Club if all three Haggersly children participated in the swim team, so they could learn strokes and get some exercise. As it turned out, only Aaron and Sophie were good at swimming. For the last two years, Robin had come home empty-handed from conference, while her siblings each took home multiple medals. Mom and Dad were always reminding Robin that because she was small, she couldn't stroke as far as the other girls. They'd insisted it didn't matter, so long as she got a Personal Best ribbon. Big whoop. In Robin's eyes, loser was loser.

This year would be different. She'd practiced all spring, and for the first time ever, she had started winning swim meets. Plus, today was her birthday. It was her turn to win a medal at conference. Had to be. Game on! This was it!

The cornfield wilderness between tiny Concord and big-city Charlotte fell away, as the brand-spanking-new, boxy, brick Aquatic Club appeared in the distance. They turned into the parking lot, weaving slowly through hundreds of swimmers and their parents. As Robin hopped out, her dad asked, "You sure you're up to this?"

"Yup!" Robin chucked her ice pack on the seat of the van, just to prove it.

By the time they'd registered, Robin regretted throwing away the ice pack. Her eye had swollen until she could barely see and strapping goggles over it was a lesson in misery.

"Ow. Ow. OWWW!!!" Robin swatted away the goggles. "I'll put them on when I absolutely have to."

Her mom took the goggles, her eyes soft with concern. "Honey, even if you get them on, I'm worried that diving will feel like knocking heads all over again. Coach said Sophie could swim for you in the relay, if you want."

Robin shook her head. The Eastcliff Breakers had won the conference title for twenty straight years. Their four-person relay teams always took first place, a surefire medal. It had taken Robin three years to qualify. And now Coach wanted her eight-year-old sister to swim in her place? Was she that bad? "I'm fine. I'll do it," Robin insisted.

"Okay," her mom replied, but Robin detected a don't-say-I-didn't-warn-you hitch in her voice. "Where is Sophie? I still need to write her events on her arm." She headed off toward the bobbing, black swim caps of the eight and unders.

At the benches, teammate and BFF Wrenn pounded her fists together, grinning, as Robin did the same.

Their synchronized ritual ended with a high, double bump of fists. "Happy b— Whoa! What'd you do to your eye?" Wrenn asked.

"Bonked heads with Sophie," Robin admitted.

Wrenn wrinkled her nose. "Youch."

Meanwhile, Jasmine let out an audible sigh before sliding onto the bench next to Robin. For some reason, Jasmine always went out of her way to make Robin feel bad. Now she leaned forward and said, "Quite an eye, Robin."

"Uhh ... thanks," Robin shot back, wondering what you're supposed to say when someone compliments your injury.

"This is the heat final for the nine–ten girls medley relay," the announcer declared. Robin knew she was eligible to swim in this, even though she had just turned eleven.

As they all rose, Jasmine said, "Hope it doesn't ruin your swimming. Be a shame for the rest of us. Right, Wrenn?"

Wrenn shrugged. "We're at conference. Not the Olympics."

Wrenn and Robin split left while Jasmine and Gina, the fourth member of their team, split right for the opposite end of the pool. Gina plunged into the water for the backstroke leg of the relay and grabbed the bar, while Robin headed for the block at the other end. A beep and a flash and Gina was off. Robin carefully strapped on her goggles, wincing with pain, and took the block. She cheered mightily as Gina took a two-stroke lead. Her turn was coming up.

As Gina touched the wall, Robin dove. At impact, her head felt like it was cracking open. She did her best to recover, bobbing and stroking as fast as she could—see the water, see the wall—but all she could see was Jasmine screaming at her. She couldn't hear anything Jasmine was saying over the dull roar of sweaty, cheering parents huddled around the edges of the pool, but Robin guessed she was behind. At last she touched the wall, and Jasmine sprang, a sneer visible on her face until she disappeared beneath the water and bobbed, her arms winging high for the butterfly leg. Robin glanced around, as her dad offered a hand to pull her out.

"Hey, Shorty! You did good."

Robin scowled at him. "I was slow."

Her dad's warm brown eyes met hers. "You're one person on a four-man team. Let's have another look at that eye." He grinned. "Wow. That's quite a bruise. You feel okay?"

Robin nodded as thunderous clapping erupted around them. The freestyle swimmers in the lanes on either side of her were just slapping the wall. Wrenn was still stroking. Robin turned to the scoreboard.

Fourth. They'd come in fourth. Not good enough for a medal.

dripping Wrenn made her way around the pool. She offered her fists again and said, "Good race," to reassure her, but Robin felt bad anyway.

Her dad dug in his pocket and handed her two bucks. "Here. Go get yourself a treat. You deserve it for racing like that. I gotta watch Sophie now."

"Thanks, Daddy." She hustled through the maze of chairs and parents who crowded the edge of the pool, as she tried to decide between Xtremes and Sour Skittles.

"Hey, Robin."

A pleasant quiver went up her spine. Jason was standing beside the smoothie bar. He knew it was her birthday—he must've come to see her!

All the girls in her fifth-grade class liked Jason. But it was Robin he called, the last day of school and every day since. She did a quick personal inventory as he walked over—her eye! OMG! Her hand whipped up to cover her bruise. "Jason!" She flashed a smile, wishing she'd at least taken off her swim cap. She was sure she looked like a gnome. "What are you doing here?"

"Uh, well." Jason looked away, awkward. What was his deal? Jasmine's father, Mr. Patterson, planted his hands proudly on Jason's shoulders, as if Jason was his son.

"This guy just had to see Jasmine swim. So we brought him."

"Oh." He wanted to see Jasmine swim? He'd come

with her parents—as in, Jasmine's *date*? He'd been calling Robin for weeks. Heart pounding, she pulled her towel closer, hugging herself.

Mr. Patterson peered closer. "Say, that's quite a shiner. How'd you get that?"

Robin's hand flew up to cover her eye again. She felt stupid. And ugly. She spotted Jasmine walking toward them, peeling away her swim cap, and shaking out her lush, blonde hair. Robin didn't feel like facing them together. She turned to go, but Jasmine called, "Robin!" in a suspiciously friendly voice. Jasmine hustled over and announced breathlessly, "You broke a record!"

"I did?" Robin asked, incredulous.

Jasmine nodded brightly and turned to Jason to explain. "Breakers hasn't lost the medley relay in twenty years. Twenty. But Robin did it! We didn't even place!"

Walked into that one. Heat itched at the back of Robin's neck as she whispered, "I gotta go."

Jason called after her, "You did a good job." But his apologetic look told her everything she needed to know—no more phone calls. She was dumped.

"Thanks," she choked out. She turned away from him, only to run into Aaron. Her big brother had seen the whole exchange.

He looked at Robin and shrugged. "Probably shoulda let Soph swim the relay, 'cause of your eye and all," he said indifferently.

She didn't want candy anymore. She was pretty sure if she ate anything, she'd throw up. She spent her dad's two bucks on Skittles and gave them to a hovering six-year-old, before going to the girls' bathroom to hide.

Twenty years? Maybe she should've given up her spot on the relay team. She'd screwed up and cost everybody a medal. But she'd wanted to win, so much— to win something cool—besides a geeky geography bee. *That* had only earned her the nickname "Hermione" at school. She just wanted to feel special.

In the bathroom stall, Robin sucked in a breath and did what she always did when things got tough: she focused on the positives. She had plenty of races left. She could still win a medal. Breaststroke was her specialty. Plus, it was her birthday. Sleepover. Wrenn. All good.

She gathered her nerve and marched out.

Drips of sweat beaded on Robin's forehead as she made her way to the van. No WAY was she going to watch the awards ceremony. Aaron was getting no less than FIVE medals and even Sophie was getting one. Meanwhile, for a THIRD year in a row, she was getting NOTHING.

Her dad was walking steadily behind her. He'd insisted on following her to the van. She could tell he was trying to think of something consoling to say, so she was ready when he offered, "Hey, champ. You did great! That eye ..."

Robin pushed him away. "I did NOT do great! I came in sixth!" Bad enough she'd lost the medley relay for the team, but then she lost the individual breaststroke competition, too! She stomped her feet, looking for something to kick, ignoring the tears that were rolling down her cheeks. She'd come in sixth. "Who wants a ribbon that says sixth? Nobody! Aaron wins everything, school stuff AND sports. All he has to do is walk in and all of mom's computer clients are like, 'Ooh! Aaron!'" She mimicked their high-pitched voices and mincing expressions. "And Sophie's beautiful. If we walk Kitty around the block, Sophie can be sucking on a tomato, seeds and juice all over her, but some old lady will still say, 'Aren't you the prettiest little girl I've ever seen!'"

Robin pointed accusingly at her dad. "You told me if I worked hard, it would pay off. And I believed you! But I didn't win anything. I'm no good at swimming, or . . . anything! I'm just ordinary." She crumbled. "I'm not getting a medal, and Jason . . . All the kids think I'm a joke . . . and I have a black eye!" She pushed her bruised face up into his.

"Shorty, you're a winner in my book, so you're going out like a winner." He lifted her on his shoulders and carried her the rest of the way to the van.

They waited in the parking lot for what felt like hours for Sophie and Aaron. Aaron had so many medals around his neck they jangled. He reminded Robin of a cow with a bell. Meanwhile her mom insisted on talking privately to her dad outside the van. Minutes later, Dad plopped back in the driver seat, heaved a sigh, and announced, "I'm up for giving the birthday girl her present now. How about you guys?" Without waiting for an answer, he passed Robin a small box. She didn't feel like being bought off, but . . . it was time for her party, after all. She opened it and stared in amazement at a cell phone. "For real? My own?" she cried.

"Happy birthday, honey. Who're you calling?" Her mom asked.

"Wrenn!" She punched in Wrenn's number and added it as number one on her speed dial.

"Um, about that. Robin, just a second, I have to tell you something. Stop dialing! I'm afraid we've had to postpone your sleepover." Robin's mouth fell open in disbelief. Her mom held up a swim cap. "At the meet we found out your sister's got head lice." She smiled sheepishly. "I'm afraid I need to check your head."

Instead of a birthday dinner and sleepover with her BFF, Robin crunched on delivery pizza that was as tasty as a Styrofoam cup, while her mom dug a painful metal comb through her scalp. Meanwhile her dad called everyone she knew to alert them to "the situation," advising them to check their own kids' heads. Mom tried to convince Robin to cut her hair short, but she placed a protective hand over her head. "Nuh-uh. No way."

She was the lone holdout. Dad and Aaron had avoided torture by shaving their heads the minute they walked in the house. Even Mom and Sophie chopped theirs short. But Robin figured if she couldn't have a birthday or a boyfriend or a medal, she should at least be allowed her *hair*. She sat at the computer reading her Facebook page while her mom yanked and pulled.

Jasmine had already posted the Haggersly Head Lice Scandal on her wall, the place on Facebook where you posted stuff so all your friends could read it. "DAD!" Robin moaned. "Why did you tell Jasmine?"

"Oh, honey, she has a right to know, you guys were swimming together," said Robin's mom. "You might have switched caps by mistake."

Robin wasn't listening, too fixated on why Jasmine referred to her as the GUO in her post. She needed to know what GUO meant, right away. She hit Google for a slang dictionary. GUO—the Great Unlucky One.

Funny, that's just how she felt.

Robin had wanted a Facebook account so much, and suddenly she couldn't remember why. Facebook only allowed kids thirteen and older to open accounts, but after she kept using Aaron's, he'd opened an account for her and simply lied about her birth date. When her mom found out, she'd threatened to shut it down until Aaron showed her that lots of kids at the middle school did the same thing. Now Robin wished her mom had closed it, because Jasmine's public humiliation was too much.

She caught her reflection in the screen and stared at her black eye and her head full of bugs. Even if she weren't a mess, she'd still be Robin, as ordinary as the backyard bird that inspired her name.

"Finished," her mom declared. She put down the comb, headed to the kitchen, and called out, "Cake!" Robin reluctantly followed. While her mom lit the candles, Dad, Aaron, and Sophie gathered around. They started to sing "Happy Birthday" but all Robin could do was stare at their almost-bald heads, barely managing to suppress her tears.

Seeing her misery, her mom reassured her, "Honey, we'll make it up to you."

Robin looked at her mother. Would there be some cool parental offering to make up for her disastrous day? Her mom continued, "I had your dad pick up strawberries and cream at the store. So I declare tomorrow Wimbledon Day. It's only the opening matches, but we'll curl up on the sofa and watch the whole thing, just like we used to."

Robin tried to muster something to say. *Wimbledon Day?* Her mom had played tennis through college, and as a result she loved the famous British tennis tournament. So when they were little, she created

"Wimbledon Day" in the hope of getting them interested. They'd dress up in tennis outfits, eat strawberries and cream, pick favorite players, and talk in phony British accents. It was fun when Robin was, like . . . five. Wimbledon Day? That would make up for . . . what?

"I don't want any stupid Wimbledon Day," she choked.

Her dad raised his voice. "Robin, that's enough!"

Her mom touched his arm. "That's fine. Why don't you just make a wish?"

The candles dripped onto the icing as Robin deliberated. What could she possibly wish? She wanted to wake up the next day and learn all her problems were gone. But since Robin Haggersly's problems weren't going to disappear, she didn't want to be Robin Haggersly anymore.

I wish I was somebody else, Robin wished. And in that moment, she meant it. She blew out the candles.

chapter two

Fiona Walker of London, England

ROBIN WOKE TO THE SENSATION OF SOMEONE shaking the bed. Who was doing that? Her mom never did that. A deep voice was saying, "Fi. Fi. FIONA WALKER."

She didn't know that voice. She had no idea who Fiona Whatever-He-Said was, either. He didn't even talk like an American. She opened her eyes to a room she didn't recognize and a balding, pudgy older man in billowing, striped pants standing over her. She sprang up and screamed.

He grinned. "Ah, good, you're up, luv. Wakey, wakey, eggs and bakey!" He tapped the doorway and headed off down the hall, singing to himself.

Robin looked around in confusion. This wasn't her room. Where was she? She didn't even remember going to bed the night before. Did they go someplace afterward? Whose room was this? Who was the man in the billowing pants? Why did he call her Fiona?

As she stood up, she caught sight of someone in the mirror. She spun around—no one. Turning back to the

20

mirror, she saw a girl about her age standing there in the reflection. Robin stepped to the right. The girl in the mirror did, too. With a shaking finger, she reached out and touched the glass. It was definitely her finger doing the touching—she could feel the glass and see the chalky trail of dust she left.

"Freaky," she whispered.

The face in the mirror was pretty—*really* pretty—with high cheekbones, ivory skin, violet eyes, and straight, raven-black hair in a blunt but stylish cut that framed her perfect neck. Her nose tilted slightly upward, like a pig's snout—but otherwise she was drop-dead gorgeous. And tall! She had to be a full head and a half taller than Robin had ever been. Not to mention breasts! Finally! She'd actually *need* to wear a bra. Robin turned to the side, admiring her unfamiliar, almost teenage shape. She noticed her pudgy little hands had been replaced by long, lean fingers on delicate wrists. And nails! Manicured, painted ruby red. Robin couldn't resist tucking one hand thoughtfully on her chin, like the models she'd seen in *Seventeen*. She waved. The girl in the mirror waved back. Robin grew dizzy.

She wasn't Robin Haggersly anymore. She was the girl in the mirror.

"Eleven is a magical number," her grandma had told her. She'd had an eleventh birthday, and she'd made a wish. And now she was Somebody Else—someone named Fiona Walker. It was like that movie she'd watched on the Disney Channel, *Freaky Friday*. She was in Fiona's body, so Fiona must be in hers. Robin silently apologized to Fiona, certain a girl this pretty couldn't possibly be happy with Robin's mouse-brown hair, brown eyes, and limited height.

But what if Fiona wasn't in her body? What if she—Robin Haggersly—didn't exist anymore? What about her mom and dad? Would they remember her and miss her? What if they didn't remember her at all? A whimper escaped her throat, even as Robin sternly instructed herself not to panic. Right now, she was Fiona Walker, and she needed to deal with that reality.

But who was Fiona Walker? Where did she live? Robin tore herself away from the mirror to regard the room. Three faded yellow walls had a foot-wide border all the way across. The eye-level border looked like an art project: cuttings from magazines, personal photographs, and ticket stubs were all welded together with tape, staples, and tacks. The whole thing was seriously cool—the real Fiona must've spent years putting it together—and Robin intended to copy the idea just as soon she got home. But first Robin had to figure out where home was, in relation to where she was now. She pored over the pictures, but the only face she recognized was the man who'd stood in her doorway minutes ago.

The man's voice called up the stairs. "FIONA! BREKKY!"

Knowing she was running out of time, Robin headed for the window and stumbled. She wasn't used to having long legs. She felt like Bambi, wobbling around. She peered out, looking for her own house in the distance. Never really having lived anywhere but Concord—except for her family's annual beach vacation—she expected to see a street she knew. But wherever Fiona Walker lived, it wasn't Concord, North Carolina.

The day was gray and misty, as if the air itself was made from a saturated sponge. Rows of unfamiliar brownstone town houses huddled around a small, square park that was lush with grass and gardens planted with gigantic, perfect, red and pink roses.

Robin stood on tiptoe, trying to see farther. More town houses—and shops! Off in the distance, she could see church spires and skyscrapers. She was in a city—a big one—unlike any she'd ever known. The streets and buildings were old, beautiful, like out of a storybook— what her mother would've called "quaint." Even the street signs were weird. At the corner, a crosswalk was painted in black and orange stripes, illuminated against the misty day by a flashing orange light.

Although Robin was mesmerized by what she saw, she was scared. Where was she, and how was she going to get home, let alone back into her body? She shut her eyes for a moment and whispered, "I wish I was Robin Haggersly of Concord, North Carolina, again."

Her wish was interrupted by the old man's urgent voice. "FI!"

Robin opened her eyes and sighed. The magic that had brought her here was not working, and she no idea why, or what else to try. But an adult might. She decided she should just get dressed and tell that man downstairs who she was and where she lived. She yanked on a pair of jeans that were slightly too short for her new, long legs and pulled a T-shirt over her head. It had the emblem of a British flag with a safety pin stuck through it. Not something she'd normally pick out, but she wasn't normal today, was she? She sucked in a deep breath and headed downstairs.

The stairs led directly to a front hall where an antique sideboard dripped in unopened bills and mail. Not even the junk mail had been thrown away. The yellowed wallpaper curled in the corners. Robin could just envision her mother walking through the door, dumping the junk mail and ripping off the wallpaper before she'd as much as said hello to the owners. Robin pushed away her sudden longing for her mom as a quick thought flashed through her brain.

Mail! Mail would have an address. She could figure out where she was. Robin glanced around, feeling like a spy as she looked at the address on a bill:

MR. NIGEL WALKER

23 BRONDESBURY VILLAS

QUEEN'S PARK, LONDON

London? She was in London, ENGLAND? How did THAT happen? Yup, she was definitely in some SERIOUS trouble when she got home. Dizzy, she followed the smell of eggs into the kitchen.

A tiny woman with impossibly long, curling red hair was at the stove. The man with the billowing pants sat at the table, newspaper in hand. He lifted his head and smiled. "Ah! There you are, darling. Tea?"

Robin nodded, unsure of what to say or even what her voice would sound like. Would her voice be her own, or Fiona's?

"Petra! Can you get Fi a cuppa?" The redheaded woman turned, her swishy purple skirt twirling with her. She looked like a gypsy, Robin thought. Or at least what she figured a gypsy would look like. The woman smiled as though she could hear Robin's thoughts and plonked a mug of tea in front of her. The man nodded approvingly and said, "Cheers, luv."

Cheers? Why was he toasting? Confused, Robin raised her mug. He looked at her quizzically, lifted his mug, and clinked it with hers. He wadded up the paper into quarters and shoved an article at her. "Reviewer's at it again. Look at this." He held it up and read mockingly, "'Circus is a Three-Ring Mess.'" He threw the paper down. "Bloody tossers, the lot of them. Don't know art when it's stuck up their bum."

Petra crowed from the stove. "I've said it before and I'll say it again. Critics are failed artists who want to make everyone as miserable as they are. The show was lovely, darling." She started singing at the stove:

> *"Magic and whimsy*
> *Is all that I make."*

The man joined in:

> *"Three rings of miracles*
> *None of them fake!"*

Petra moved to the table and clasped his hands as he rose to meet her. They sang together:

> *"Acrobats, animals, on with the show!*
> *How can I be else when it's all that I know!*
> *The circus is all that I KNOW!!!"*

Petra hit a high note with the finale as the man dipped her. Her spatula waved in the air and they both laughed.

Robin stared at them in amazement. She'd never seen anyone sing at breakfast. And they were good, too! Like professional good! But weird. Really, really weird. She glanced at the review. On the page was a picture of the two of them with a caption:

DIRECTOR NIGEL WALKER AND

HIS LEADING-LADY WIFE, PETRA.

So Fiona's mom was an actress, and her dad was a director. How cool was that? Okay, they were a little weird, singing in the kitchen, but the article even mentioned television shows they'd done! Maybe, when Robin switched back with Fiona, and she was Robin again, maybe they'd be so grateful they'd put her in a show.

Robin shook herself out of the daydream. Right now, what she needed to do was get back to her own body. And she needed help to do that.

Mrs. Walker set a plate of eggs in front of her. "Now then, eat up. Jo's got footie. If we hurry we can just catch the second half."

Robin picked up the fork and poked at the eggs, her face burning with embarrassment. She was scared to tell them. What if they thought she was crazy, or what if telling someone messed up whatever magic would take her home? But what choice did she have? Robin let her fork drop onto the plate, sucked in a breath, and admitted, "I can't." The sound threw her, not only because her voice was low and throaty, but because she

27

sounded like them. The word *can't* came out "cahhhn't."

Mr. Walker sipped his tea. "Can't? Can't what?"

Robin tried again. "I can't go...." What was "footie" anyway? She tried to finish her thought. "I can't go ... wherever you're going."

Petra sighed. "Why not? I thought you wanted us to be more normal, Fi. Wasn't that what we were arguing about last night? This is normal. Sunday football and lunch at the pub."

Robin shook her head. "You don't understand." There it was again—"understahhhhnd!" Why was she talking this way? She sounded like she was British. In desperation she blurted out, "I'm not Fiona Walker."

Mr. Walker stopped eating, intrigued. "Really? Who are you, then?"

He wasn't making fun of her, she was sure of it. His eyes were kind and his voice was sincere. Still, she hesitated. What would happen if she told? Having no idea what else to do, Robin took a deep breath and began.

"My name is Robin Haggersly. I live at 161 North Union Street in Concord, North Carolina. It was my birthday last night. I made a wish—I just wanted to get away from being me—and I woke up here, in Fiona's body. I don't know you. I've never seen either of you. I've never even been to England. I need your help to get home. Can you call my mom? I can give you our number. Please help me."

Mr. and Mrs. Walker looked at her for a long moment and then started laughing. Mr. Walker clapped his hands. "Bloody marvelous, Fi!"

Mrs. Walker nodded her approval. "Your delivery was excellent, dahling. Where did you find that monologue? Or did you just make it up?"

Robin stared in disbelief. What were these people talking about? She shook her head violently. "I'm not Fiona. I'm not even British—"

But she sounded British. And she looked like Fiona Walker. She spoke again, laboring over each word so she sounded like an American. She had to sound like an American to convince them, but for some reason, that was suddenly hard to do.

"I'm SEE-REE-OUS. I ahm—I mean, I AM Robin Haggersly. I don't know where Fiona is, but she's not HEEERE." Robin gulped and smiled apologetically at the Walkers. "Maybe if you can help me get home, she'll come back, too."

Mr. Walker grinned. "Ah! Not breaking character yet, are we?"

Robin sagged. They thought she was acting out a part. Mr. Walker glanced at the clock on the wall. "Well, Robin-Haggersly-Who-Used-to-be-Fiona-Walker," he started again, "tell you what. We'll go to your sister's game and pick you up afterward for the pub. If you still need to find your way to Kansas, we'll work on it." He picked up his keys. "Ready, Petra?"

29

Mrs. Walker sighed again. "Sure you're not coming, Fi?"

Robin started to protest, but shook her head instead. They headed out, Mr. Walker singing "Somewhere Over the Rainbow." Mrs. Walker harmonized, their voices echoing until the front door swung shut.

Once Robin was certain she was alone in the house, she closed her eyes and did a quick inventory of the situation. Okay, she'd switched bodies by accident, but that probably meant she could switch back. In the meantime, the Walkers seemed like really nice people. Plus, she was in England! How cool was that?

First thing she needed to do was make sure her body was still there—that Robin Haggersly still existed.

She spotted a phone on the kitchen wall. She had no idea how to call home from England, so she hit "0" and got the operator. In her most grown-up voice, she gave the operator her home phone number. The phone rang many times. Robin worried her parents were at church, until a muffled voice finally answered. "He . . . Hello?" Her mom was groggy. Why would she be asleep in the middle of the day?

"Mummy?" Robin wrinkled her nose. Why was she saying "Mummy?" Her lips had formed the word *Mommy*, but it had come out all wrong.

Her mom's drowsy voice quickly said, "Wrong number," and hung up.

Robin dialed again. This time her mom picked up on the first ring, mumbled, "Wrong number again." *Click!* Robin decided she needed a story. After all, even Mr. Walker thought she was Fiona. She needed to be someone her mom would listen to—a grown-up. On inspiration, she called again. This time, her mom sounded angry.

"Who is this?"

"Mrs. Haggersly? This is the British Police." Robin knew "British Police" was probably wrong. She'd heard the correct term before, but she couldn't remember right now. She thought fast. "If you check your caller ID, you will see that I am calling from London, England." Robin held her breath. Her mom paused, probably pulling the phone away to look.

"Yes?" Robin could hear hesitation creeping into her voice.

Robin lowered her voice. "Yes, ma'am. We have a young lady here who claims to be your daughter. A Miss Robin Haggersly?"

"What? That's impossible."

"Oh no, I assure you, ma'am, that it's not. She's right here. Pretty girl, but I'm sorry to say she has a nasty case of head lice."

HA! That should get her mother's attention! Robin almost gurgled with pleasure when she heard her mother's footsteps over the phone. Finally! Most likely she was going to check Robin's room. Robin quickly continued, "Yes, ah, Robin says she made a wish to be somebody else, and she woke up here in England. Now she's at the home of a Mr. Nigel Walker...."

Her mom cut in, tense. "I don't know who this is, or what kind of a stunt you're pulling, but you're not Scotland Yard. And my daughter is right here, in her bed, as she should be at FIVE A.M. on SUNDAY MORNING." She hung up the phone.

Oops. Robin had forgotten there was a time difference between England and America. Some geography bee champ she was.

Time for Plan B.

Robin wandered the Walker house again, this time in search of the computer. She had to brush aside the old newspapers, coffee mugs, and cereal bowls that littered every room. The Walkers obviously didn't care as much about cleaning as her mom did. After tossing aside an abandoned T-shirt and sweatpants, she finally found an aging PC at a desk in the living room. Keeping one eye on the front door in case the Walkers returned, Robin switched it on. An icon in the corner indicated the email address of one Fiona Walker. Robin clicked on it, hoping she wouldn't need a password. No such luck.

Robin tried variations of Fiona's name for the password—fwalker, fionaw—nothing. She checked around the desk, hoping to find the password stuck on a Post-it or a piece of scratch paper. After five minutes of rooting around, she slammed the drawer shut, aggravated. Fiona Walker was just plain old rude. At least Robin had the decency to leave her email open at her home in North Carolina. Because who knew when someone else might wake up in your body and need to use it! Fiona could click on Robin's icon—anytime—and read. No password required.

Wait a minute.

Robin blushed when she realized how obvious the solution was: she didn't need Fiona's email address. She had her *own*. She opened her email Web site and logged on as Robin Haggersly. She hit COMPOSE before pausing. What should she say? What do you write to yourself?

After several tries, Robin finally settled for:

To: rhaggersly@carolina.rr.com
Fr: rhaggersly@carolina.rr.com
Hi. If I said I used to be Robin Haggersly, would that mean something to you?
Sincerely,
Used-to-be-Robin
P.S. Fiona, if this is you, I don't have your email password. So just send a reply at rhaggersly and tell me if you're me!

Nodding with satisfaction, Robin clicked SEND, just as she heard the front door rattle. The Walkers were back. She rose from the computer, convinced that she and Fiona would find a way together. Right now, the only thing she could do was wait for a reply. But how *long* would she have to wait? A day, a week...or a year?

chapter three

Neera Gupta of Gawa, India

ROBIN GRIPPED THE DOOR HANDLE OF MR. Walker's tiny, dented hatchback as the car whizzed around the corner. Logically, she knew English people drove on the other side of the road, but that didn't make the actual drive any less heart-stopping. She caught her breath with every right turn, past oncoming traffic. As she saw more and more cars pass peacefully by, she finally managed to take a look around. As disturbed as she was at being Fiona Walker, she couldn't help marveling that she really was in England! She figured she'd better appreciate everything she could, since she planned on going home as quickly as possible.

The car screeched to a halt in front of a pub named "The Slug and Lettuce." Mr. Walker shifted back and forth, parking inventively over half of the sidewalk, ignoring hostile glances from people eating at the outdoor tables. He leapt out energetically and yanked back the seat. "Right. Shall we?" Petra Walker took his arm, while Robin and Jo Walker climbed out.

Sixteen-year-old Jo, still dressed in a soccer uniform, hadn't said a word in the car. When the Walkers had stopped by the house to pick up Robin, she'd been excited to see that Jo was a girl—she'd always wanted an older sister! But Jo had wrinkled her nose at the sight of Robin and sat as far away from her as the tiny backseat would allow. She proceeded to pick the mud out of her cleats, indifferently dropping the dirt and grass on the seat and, occasionally, on Robin.

As they walked inside, Robin ogled the pub while the patrons ogled the Walkers. Fiona's parents did look a bit out of place: Mrs. Walker's long, flowing red hair, swirling purple skirt, and peacock feather earrings looked positively exotic next to the ordinary Sunday dresses of the other women. Mr. Walker's billowing, striped pants and ruffled shirt were also a bit unusual, compared with the suits the other men wore. Only Jo fit in with the scenery, but she quickly abandoned Robin, taking the last chair at a table next to them, one full of teenage girls in matching uniforms.

Robin had heard of pubs, but she'd never really understood what made them special. They looked just like American bars: with a tall mahogany bar crowded with stools, wooden beams, Tiffany lamps, and a big-screen TV. But glancing around, Robin realized the difference: everyone came to the pub. Families poured through the door, parents making their way to the bar while their kids split right and left, weaving around the seats to the tables. Teens like Jo sat in the corners, their legs kicked up on the table as they scowled at passersby. College-age guys stood in front of the TV, dark foamy drinks in hand, slapping backs and cheering at the "footie." Robin had learned in the car that footie was what English people called soccer. Even elderly people were here, still dressed in church clothes, complete with hat and gloves.

Mr. Walker picked out a table by the window. He rocked from one leg to the other as he checked his wallet for cash. "Right. Now, darlings, what do you fancy?"

Guessing he was offering her a drink, Robin answered dubiously. "Um, Sprite?"

Mr. Walker grinned. "Ah. So I see Robin Haggersly is still with us. Right you are, a Sprite for the American." He turned to Mrs. Walker, speaking with an imitation cowboy accent. "What do you say, darling? A Bud for the little missus?"

Mrs. Walker chuckled but then replied, "Leave off, Nigel, get the babe a lemonade. I'll have a Shandy."

Nigel looked over at his eldest daughter. "Jo?"

Jo shrugged and looked at her friends. "I'll pass, thanks."

"Right you are. Back in a tick." Mr. Walker wandered off to the busy bar, as a shy-looking piano player raised his eyebrows at Mrs. Walker. She nodded demurely and rose.

Jo rolled her eyes. Pushing off the table with her feet, she leaned her chair all the way back to mutter in Robin's ear, "Here we go." Mrs. Walker cued the piano player and started singing some old-time show tune, complete with jazz hands and hip bumps. Robin listened appreciatively, until Jo scowled and interrupted.

"So what's this now, runt? You're an American?"

Robin startled at the name "runt." It sounded mean—especially now that she was so tall—but she decided to ignore it. For all Robin knew, it might be a term of affection between the two sisters. Anyway, it was more important to figure out whether she should try telling Fiona's older sister the truth. So far, the truth hadn't worked out too well. She shrugged. "It's just a joke I'm playing." She balked at saying that the joke was on Jo's parents. She just couldn't bring herself to call Mr. Walker her dad.

Jo grinned with relief. "Phew. For a moment there, I thought you'd gone all toady on me."

Robin fumbled, "Err . . . what do you mean?"

"You know. Like them." Jo gestured with her head toward Mrs. Walker, wrapping up her song with a dramatic bow, while Mr. Walker whistled and pumped his fist like he was at a boxing match. Robin silently rehearsed "toady" to remind herself it meant uncool. Who knew it was so hard to speak English in England?

Jo looked at her strangely. "Why do you keep wiggling? Got something in your knickers?"

Robin looked at her blankly. She always wiggled. It was just the way she was. Unable to think of an answer, she concentrated on sitting still and staring at the TV.

The college guys changed the channel—Wimbledon. Robin groaned. Jo's parents weren't the only ones capable of being toady. At least this little adventure got her out of Wimbledon Day. On the other hand, was her mom doing Wimbledon Day without her? Robin briefly tried to imagine Fiona waking up in her body, having to face Wimbledon Day with her family: Fiona would be a British girl, pretending to be an American girl, pretending to be British. She grew dizzy just thinking about it.

Mr. Walker picked his way to the table, his hands full of drinks. "Jo! Dartboard's open! Grab it, would you? Let's have a game!" He turned toward Robin. "'Cause I'm feeling LUCKY!" He called to the small stage. "Petra! Game on!" Mrs. Walker nodded, took a last bow, and stepped down, while Mr. Walker placed his hands on Robin's shoulders and steered her to the back of the pub. Robin felt his excitement. Finally, something fun! And really British, too!

Two older men were just putting the darts back in their cases. Mr. Walker called out, "Hang on a sec, gents, I'll have that." They nodded and handed the darts to Mr. Walker as he muttered "cheers" again. Apparently "cheers" was "thank you." The old men smiled at Robin and she smiled shyly back.

Mr. Walker was as exuberant as ever. "What's teams? I call Fi!"

Jo sniffed. "Of course you do."

The old men looked at Robin. "Is the young one really good, then?" one of them asked.

This time Mr. Walker sniffed. "Slug champion last year, actually." The term *champion* took Robin by surprise.

The old men raised their eyebrows. "You don't say." They folded their arms and waited, intent on watching.

Mr. Walker grinned at Jo. "Usual stakes, then?"

Jo shrugged. "It's your funeral." She turned toward her mother and passed her a handful of darts. "Mum, you're up." Petra Walker fired three swift shots—all of which landed near the bull's-eye. Mr. Walker and Jo followed suit, casually tossing darts with the accuracy of sharpshooters.

Robin suppressed her nervousness. Champion darts player? Her? She'd never played a game of darts in her life. Sure, she'd tossed the darts at the board in Aaron's room, but she didn't even know how to score an actual game. She threw and the shots went wide, one even bouncing off the board and onto the table. The old men suppressed smirks, as Mr. Walker grimaced and picked up the darts. He looked at Robin. "No matter. Just have to get your game face on."

They went in rounds, and gradually Robin eased into the game. On her third turn, she tossed one on number 19. Mr. Walker clapped his hands and regarded her with pride. "That's my girl!" As he strutted past the old men, he couldn't resist bragging, "Going to be my little star next week!"

One of the old gentlemen piped up. "What's that, then?" Mr. Walker answered, but Robin couldn't hear.

Jo's face became cross. "You've got to be kidding me. You quit."

Robin was blank. "What?"

The older Walkers laughed, like she'd told a great joke, but Jo stared her down. She hissed, "You quit, Fi. Last night. You swore to me." At Robin's blank look, Jo walked over, ripped a poster off the wall, and stuck it in Robin's face. On the poster was Fiona Walker in a dainty, old-fashioned, long blue dress, next to a sprightly young Peter Pan. "Are you playing Wendy or not?"

Mrs. Walker smacked her hand on a table. "She never said she wouldn't do it, Jo, stop putting words into her mouth! We all agreed—"

"After! She told me this after the fight in the kitchen! Upstairs!" Jo shouted. She turned to Robin and demanded, "Tell them!"

Robin's mouth opened and closed, but she had no idea what to say. She hadn't told Jo anything—the real Fiona Walker had, and who knew what she'd said. Robin, meanwhile, was still processing the idea of starring in a play. She'd never even been onstage.

Jo's eyes narrowed at Robin's silence. Mrs. Walker nodded and said, "There, see, Jo? She hasn't made up her mind. There's obviously been a miscommunication between the two of you. We'll sort it out at home, later. Let's finish the game. Still your turn, Fi. FI!"

Robin snapped to attention and picked up the dart, as a glaring Jo mouthed the word, "Payback." The blood drained from Robin's face as she let the dart go. They all turned at Mr. Walker's shout, as the dart landed firmly in his rear end.

While Mr. Walker was audibly moaning behind the bathroom door—his wife patiently administering first aid—Jo disappeared to the bar, and Robin reeled in her seat.

Fiona Walker was beautiful. And a darts champion. And the star of a play. But Fiona Walker wasn't here— plain old Robin Haggersly was. Unless she could get herself home ASAP, Robin could potentially ruin Fiona's life and Mr. Walker's livelihood. Being short, brown-eyed, brown-haired, lice-infested, sixth-place-swimmer Robin was NOWHERE NEAR AS BAD as standing onstage as Fiona, pretending to be Wendy in *Peter Pan* and looking like a total dork.

Mr. Walker was pale when he emerged, and Robin cast her eyes to the floor. Mrs. Walker smiled brightly at her. "No matter, luv. Pop's all right. Ready to go, then?"

Robin started to rise when Jo called out, "Hang on!"

She slung a plate on the bar ledge. "Usual stakes, right, Dad? That means these belong to you and Fiona. On me."

Two chunks of gray, scaly fish parts, dripping in some sort of liquid, sat on the plate. The old gentlemen grinned. Mr. Walker wrinkled his nose but nodded in surrender. He picked one up. "Come on, Fi, rules are rules. Losers eat." He handed one to Robin, but it slithered out of her hand and made an ugly *splat* on the plate. Her stomach rolled. Mr. Walker said encouragingly, "Come on now. We'll do it together. Ready?" Robin picked it up again, the aroma of vinegar making her nose curl. Mr. Walker smiled at his audience. "Down in one, then." He swallowed. Robin plugged her nose before stuffing the fish into her mouth. She gagged and swallowed.

Jo grinned. "Worth it! Mmm . . . jellied eel! Sorted! Let's go home." She trotted out the door.

Following the Walkers outside, Robin felt green. Jellied eel was NOT something she was willing to eat ever again.

But at least the clock over the door said three p.m. What time was it back home? Robin did some quick calculations. She'd called home at ten o'clock in the morning, London time. Her mom had said—okay, shouted—it was five o'clock in the morning there. That meant the time difference was five hours. It was three o'clock in London, so it was ten in the morning in North Carolina. There might be an answer by now, and maybe a way home.

At the Walker home, Robin and Jo headed for the computer at the same time. Smaller and faster, Robin claimed the chair and smiled triumphantly, the taste of eel still curdling in her mouth. Jo scowled and left, as Robin opened her email and cheered out loud. It was there! An answer from herself! She read eagerly, but the answer made her reel.

> **To: rhaggersly@carolina.rr.com**
> **Fr: rhaggersly@carolina.rr.com**
> **Re: Hi**
> Hi, Robin. I don't know who Fiona is—I'm Neera Gupta. I'm from India. Last night I made a wish to be somebody else, and I was suddenly in your body, standing over a birthday cake. I don't know how this happened and I'm TOTALLY SORRY if I've caused this. Your family is really nice, but I'd like to go home now. Do you have any ideas how we can get back?
> Neera
> (P.S. your brother is REALLY cute, BTW!)

Robin's stomach rolled again. So this wasn't like *Freaky Friday*. It wasn't a straight switch. The girl in her body wasn't Fiona Walker, it was Neera Gupta. Where was Fiona? And who was in this Neera girl's body? How were they supposed to get home? Desperately hoping Neera was still online, Robin hit the IM button.

HOW OLD ARE U, NEERA?

The answer shot back in moments.

11.

ME 2. AND U'VE NEVER HEARD OF FIONA WALKER?

No.

Robin hesitated. This was the strangest conversation she'd ever had. Questions flooded into her head. Did she need to find Fiona Walker in order to make this right? Or could Robin and Neera both just wish again, right now? Or should they get help? Tell her mom together? A new panic seized Robin, and she typed furiously.

HAS THIS HAPPENED 2 U BEFORE? DID U TELL MY FAMILY?

No and no. Was too scared!!! Do you think we're supposed to?

Robin thought for a moment, trying to gauge her mother's reaction. Combined with the call Robin had made this morning, her mom might believe Neera and really freak out. Still, even if her mom did freak out, it was unlikely she could fix this.

MAYBE NOT. BTW, NEW RULE. NO CALLING MY BROTHER CUTE WHILE U'RE IN MY BODY. MAJOR EWWW.

Right. Sorry. But he is!

EW. EW. EW. NEW SUBJECT. DO U—DID U—
SPEAK ENGLISH IN INDIA?

Only a little. Not like this! For some reason, I still think
in Hindi, but I totally understand everyone talking in English
all of a sudden. And I answer them in English, too. I tried
whispering a little Hindi to myself, just to see what would
happen, but my mouth—I mean your mouth—wouldn't form
the words. And now I'm typing in English! So weird!

So that was why Robin was speaking with an
English accent. Whatever magic was working on them,
in their heads they heard their own languages, but what
came out was the language and accent of the girl whose
body they were in. She tried to think. What could they
do? She typed rapidly.

HAVE U CALLED HOME? COULD FIONA WALKER
BE IN UR BODY IN INDIA?

I haven't called—we don't have a phone. Or a
computer. I only go online at school. I went on your email
this morning because I was trying to find out about u.

Robin bit her lip, trying to get her head around
this new problem. She'd been ready to ask Fiona to
try and wish at the same time. But Fiona wasn't in
her body. Instead, Neera was, and that complicated
things. If she asked and Neera refused, it might
make their relationship a little awkward. And Robin
sensed she needed to stay on good terms with Neera.
They needed more information before they tried
anything. She wrote:

46

DO U THINK THERE ARE MORE OF US? MORE
THAN JUST YOU, ME & FIONA, I MEAN?

I guess there could be. How do we find out?

Robin paused again. How could they look for
Fiona or anyone else who might know about this?
Robin scrunched up her face, trying to think what
her mom would do. She'd probably build a Web site.
But that took money. What else did her mom do to
communicate with people?

An idea struck her.

FACEBOOK! MY PASSWORD IS LABKITTY. I'LL
OPEN AN ACCOUNT AS FIONA & REQUEST U AS A
FRIEND. CONFIRM ME & I'LL MEET YOU ON MY—
SORRY, YOUR—HOME PAGE IN ABOUT 5—THIS IS
SO CONFUSING!

Okay.

Robin opened Facebook, having no idea whether
Fiona already had an account or not. But seeing as
she didn't know Fiona's email password, she figured
she wouldn't know her Facebook one, either. She'd
just join again. She didn't know Fiona's birthday, so
she decided to follow Aaron's example and make one
up, one that would make Fiona Walker thirteen years
old, the minimum age for Facebook users. When she
was done joining, she clicked on Fiona's new home
page and friended Robin Haggersly. Neera instantly
confirmed her as a friend, and Robin started teaching
her how to use the site.

THIS IS THE WALL. EVERYBODY HAS ONE. UR WALL IS LIKE A BULLETIN BOARD—U CAN POST WHAT UR DOING OR THINKING. ALL OF UR FB FRIENDS CAN READ UR WALL, SO BE CAREFUL WHAT U WRITE, IN CASE U DON'T WANT OTHER PEOPLE TO SEE. U CAN SEND A PRIVATE MSG INSTEAD—SEE BUTTON ON LEFT THAT SAYS "LEAVE FIONA A PRIVATE MESSAGE." THAT'S LIKE AN EMAIL. ONLY I CAN SEE IT.

Got it.

COOL. NOW LOOK DOWN LEFT-HAND SIDE. U WILL SEE SOME OF MY FRIENDS LISTED—SOME HAVE GREEN CIRCLES AND SOME HAVE HALF MOONS. SEE IT?

Yes. What does that mean?

I'LL SHOW U.

Robin swung the cursor to the right-hand side, clicked on Robin Haggersly's name, and up popped a chat room. She wrote inside the chat room:

HELLO AGAIN! GREEN CIRCLE—I'M ONLINE AND U CAN CHAT ROOM ME. HALF MOON—I'M NOT.

Cool! Who is Wrenn? She's chat rooming me, too.

Robin grimaced. If she and Neera continued to use their personal pages to communicate, Wrenn and her other friends would think Robin was online and they'd keep hitting chat rooms. Plus, they'd be able to see anything Neera posted, and Robin wasn't sure whether she wanted to tell anybody about her current body mix-up, since she didn't intend to be this way for long. She wondered where she and Neera could talk privately.

She skimmed the Facebook toolbar, surveying her options. She could open a private group! Then they would have a very private wall, where they could talk freely about their situation. Robin clicked on the option and paused. What should they call themselves? The only thing Robin knew about Neera was that she'd wished, same as Robin had. So she typed in *WISHERS*, then got back to Neera.

REQUEST TO BE A "FRIEND" OF WISHERS. I'LL CONFIRM U.

Neera did as instructed.

NO ONE SEES THIS XCEPT US, BECAUSE WE'RE THE ONLY MEMBERS OF THIS PRIVATE GROUP. WE CAN POST WHATEVER WE WANT, AND WHEN WE FIND MORE GIRLS LIKE US, WE CAN ADD THEM.

Cool! I feel like we're in a tree house together! Our own secret club. But how are we supposed to find other girls like us?

Neera was right. Now it was too private! How were any other Wishers—if there were any—supposed to find them? Robin thought for a minute.

HANG ON A SEC, NEERA, I'M GOING TO OPEN A PUBLIC GROUP 2.

Anybody could see a public page. If there were other Wishers out there, they could be searching public pages on Facebook right now, in hopes of finding girls just like them. Robin had learned how to open a public page on Facebook when she helped her mom establish the swim team site. She'd promised faithfully she would never, ever, do one herself, but her situation had changed. They needed to reach out to girls worldwide— girls like Fiona—whom she didn't know and had no way of knowing. She found a picture of Fiona on the shelf. Tossing the frame aside, she scanned it and then posted it on the page. Finally, Robin added her own profile picture next to Fiona's, with a caption:

HAVE YOU EVER WISHED TO BE SOMEBODY ELSE?
AND DID THAT WISH COME TRUE? DID YOU WAKE UP AND LOOK
IN THE MIRROR AND NOT KNOW WHO YOU WERE LOOKING AT?
ARE YOU ELEVEN? IF YOU ANSWERED YES TO ALL THESE
QUESTIONS, SEND US A MESSAGE.

Robin paused briefly to admire her work, then returned to Neera on the Wisher page.

OKAY, HERE'S THE DEAL. GIRLS SEE THE PUBLIC PAGE AND APPLY TO BE A FRIEND. BUT WE MIGHT GET FRIENDED BY PEOPLE WHO AREN'T LIKE US. IF WE DECIDE THEY'RE WISHERS, WE FRIEND THEM IN THE PRIVATE GROUP.

Works for me! How long do u think it will take till someone finds us?

NO IDEA. LET'S WAIT HERE FOR A WHILE JUST IN CASE.

Logically, Robin knew she needed to give her plan time to work. But she wanted to go home—if someone had information about how to do that, she intended to jump on it. While she and Neera waited in hope that someone would find their Wisher page, they asked each other questions.

WHY'D U WISH, NEERA? SECRET FACT (OR SF): I'M ALLERGIC TO YELLOW JACKETS.

Was tired of babysitting 4 little sisters and brothers. U?

U FORGOT A SF.

Oh, sorry. SF: I can't swim.

Can't swim? Oops. That was going to be a problem at the Haggersly house. Robin wrote back, answering Neera's question.

WAS TIRED OF BEING ORDINARY. WHERE DO U LIVE IN INDIA?

Gawa. It's an island. SF: I don't eat red meat. & ur dad is making hamburgers.

WOW. I'D KILL FOR A BURGER. ATE JELLIED EEL TODAY. MAJOR YUCK.

I love eel!

Huh.

At nine o'clock in England, Neera was being summoned by Robin's mom. Robin had to accept she wasn't going home, at least not tonight. She clomped upstairs to Fiona's room. She smelled fresh paint, hit the light, and stared in shock. Fiona's carefully crafted photo border was ruined; someone had painted a thick but tidy black stripe over the whole thing. Robin was horrified, thinking how much time it must have taken for Fiona to put that border together. Someone had destroyed it in less than an hour while she was on the computer.

Mr. or Mrs. Walker? Robin doubted it. They seemed really nice, plus they were artists. She felt certain they wouldn't destroy their daughter's work, even if they hated it. They certainly wouldn't be secretive about it.

Jo. Had to be. There wasn't anyone else. She'd promised Robin there would be payback. But why? Why did Jo hate her? Robin deliberated screaming for Mrs. Walker, if only in a show of loyalty to Fiona. But she guessed that was what Jolene was expecting. The older girl was ready for a fight, and Robin wasn't.

Robin decided to do nothing. She had every intention of going home the next day. Someone would find them on Facebook and would know how they could get home. And when Fiona got home, she could deal with her sister's meanness herself. Throwing on a T-shirt, Robin switched off the light and smothered her face in Fiona's pillow to stave off the paint fumes. When she couldn't fall asleep, she pretended she could feel Sophie's warm softness, cuddling up beside her.

chapter four

Alia Newport of Concord, North Carolina

WHEN ROBIN WOKE THE NEXT MORNING, the sky outside her window was a brilliant blue. It reminded Robin of the cornflower-blue crayon Sophie had once tried on Robin's wall, because she loved it so much.

It has to be cooler outside, Robin thought sleepily. *Maybe Mom will take us bike riding in the park.* She formulated a plan: Mom would probably say no at first, because of work, so she'd get Sophie to do the asking. If Sophie wanted something, she wanted it, and it was worth crying for. Her mom would most likely give in.

But even as the park near her home formed an irresistible image in her brain, something nagged at Robin's memory. She knew there was a reason why she couldn't go to the park, and it had nothing to do with her mom's work. Robin glanced around her room, trying to remember what it was.

Blackened photograph border, beanbag chair, chipped windowsill—this wasn't her room. The hushed voices downstairs were definitely too quiet to be the Haggerslys, and the brilliant blue sky outside didn't belong to North Carolina, either.

She was still Fiona Walker of London, England. She'd been Fiona Walker for one whole day, while a girl named Neera Gupta was living her life in North Carolina. And she needed to fix that.

Robin swallowed her disappointment as she threw on a pair of jeans and a striped T-shirt and scrounged for a sweater—it was surprisingly cold in the Walker house. She ran to the bathroom and scooped up the toothbrush she'd used the previous day. A Post-it note was stuck to the handle: *USE YOUR OWN, RUNT!* Robin mentally apologized for borrowing—whose, Jolene's?—toothbrush the day before. It had to be Jo's, because who else would call her runt? But where was Fiona's toothbrush? Uncertain, Robin brushed her teeth with her index finger. She hoped someone who knew something had joined their Facebook page and could tell her how to get home to her own toothbrush.

A familiar voice boomed up the stairs. "FIONA! BREKKY!" Mr. Walker.

Robin tiptoed downstairs, not wanting to alert anyone that she was awake. She needed privacy and that was hard to come by at the Walkers' house, especially when it came to the computer. They only had the one computer in the living room, and household traffic to and from it was heavy. Robin had learned the hard way last night that if she so much as got up to use the bathroom, she'd most likely find Mrs. Walker or Jo typing away when she got back. This was a problem, because Robin had decided she needed to keep the Wisher page a secret. What if Mrs. Walker sat down at the computer and saw it? Would she believe Robin's story? What would she do? Or, even worse, what if Fiona wasn't allowed to be on Facebook? Parents were funny about stuff like that and Robin couldn't risk it. Aside from her email account, Facebook was her only link to her true identity.

She logged on. Four responses! Excited, Robin clicked the first one open, then the second and third with growing disappointment. Two were from teenage girls who dreamed of getting full-body makeovers. Another was from a boy who wanted to know if Fiona dated. The last one was from Alia Newport. Alia? Why—how—had Aaron's girlfriend joined their Wisher group?

Robin felt a momentary panic. What if Alia knew? She might face a reckoning worse than when she'd set the kitchen on fire. Alia had sent Fiona a private message, too. With trepidation, Robin opened it.

Robin, I know what has happened. 1) Stop wishing. 2) Extrmly imp—is this Fiona's real bday? If not, find out what her real bday is. Write back ASAP.

Robin's fingers were trembling. How did Alia know? Had Neera told her? She must've. Had Alia told Aaron? Her parents? Why was Fiona's birthday so important? A voice interrupted her thoughts.

"What are YOU still doing here?" Startled, Robin clicked off Facebook. Petra Walker was standing in the hall, a shocked and angry look on her face. Robin froze.

Mrs. Walker grabbed a backpack next to the door and handed it to her. "It's Monday morning! We assumed when you didn't come to breakfast that you'd already left for school! Fi, you're late!" She made a tsking noise and shouted to the kitchen. "NIGEL! YOU'LL NEED TO DRIVE YOUR YOUNGEST TO SCHOOL!" She turned back to Robin. "No time left for brekky. Get your uni, would you? C'mon, luv, let's get a move on."

What was a "uni"? Robin was dazed. School? She couldn't go to school as Fiona. She had to stay by the computer and wait for Alia. She had to find out Fiona's birthday. She had no time to go to school with kids she didn't know. Heck, she didn't even know *where* to go! Robin ran through a list of possible excuses, as Mr. Walker drifted into the hall.

"What's that now?" He calmly lifted a cup of tea to his lips.

Irritated, Mrs. Walker stuffed a set of car keys into his hand and took his mug. "Fi has school today, and it started ten minutes ago."

"Does she?" Mr. Walker seemed incredulous, but Mrs. Walker's impatient sigh rattled him into action.

"Right. Let's go then, Fi. Mustn't keep Headmaster waiting." He turned to head back down the hall.

"Wait! No! How can I have school? It's summer vacation!" Robin spluttered, amazed at the simple logic of her argument. She didn't need an excuse. Clearly, the Walkers were confused. She changed her tone, gently prodding them. "It's July?"

"Ah." Mr. Walker paused. But just as Robin sensed victory, his brow wrinkled. "I had school in July."

Mrs. Walker took her by the shoulders and steered her toward the door. "As do you, Fi. Summer holidays start in two weeks' time." She sighed and looked at the clock. "Her uni—"

Mr. Walker waved it off. "Pah! Unis are for sheep, right, Fi?"

Again that word: uni. Yoo-nee. What did it mean? Robin nodded anyway. Mrs. Walker surrendered. "All right, it's late anyway, so just this once. Go with your dad, and we'll see you this afternoon." Mr. Walker gave his wife a quick peck.

"I'll be at the Haymarket for a tech run. Don't wait up." He swung the front door open and started singing:

> *"Bus stop wet day*
> *She's there I say . . ."*

In the car, Robin pleaded again. "Please, can't I just miss school today? I have a lot—"

Mr. Walker cut her off. "I don't know what you're so worried about, darling. Something wrong with the boyfriend?"

Boyfriend?

"Can't be class. You've been the top pupil at Clarendon your entire career!" He snorted. "You'll do brilliantly, you always do. You just need to stay focused." He pulled up to a nondescript brick building and kissed the top of her head. "Now out you go, there's a good girl."

Top pupil, too? As in best student? Was there anything Fiona Walker didn't do perfectly? With a sigh, Robin stepped out of the car, feeling like a piece of furniture. She didn't have any say in *where* she went as Robin Haggersly OR Fiona Walker. She was just picked up and moved around like an armchair, until the grown-ups decided yes, that's where she belonged.

Standing on the sidewalk, Robin contemplated her next move. She could skip school. She was, after all, in London. There was bound to be a coffee shop with Internet access somewhere close by. If tiny Concord, North Carolina, had one, surely London had dozens. But she had no money.

Or . . . she could attempt to sneak back to the Walker home and use the computer. She'd done her best to memorize the route, but between the speed with which Mr. Walker drove, and the many dizzying roundabouts— traffic circles—Robin doubted she could find it.

The *least* appealing idea was going to school as Fiona Walker. She could claim amnesia. Like she'd hit her head and forgotten who she was, who her teacher was, what grade she was in, and where she was supposed to go. She'd look like a doof.

Mr. Walker reversed wildly back to where she was standing, rolling down the window. He leaned out, waving a small object, "Fi. Your phone? Looks like you haven't checked it all weekend." He peeled out.

She had a phone! She could call Alia! Robin instantly started dialing, determined to retrieve Alia's home number from an operator. It was four a.m. there, but she didn't care. She *had* to talk to Alia, right now. But the call would not go through. She pressed furiously on the buttons, as a high-pitched, wobbly voice interrupted her.

"Miss Walker?" A pinched-faced man in a navy suit was walking down the steps, straightening his tie. "I trust you are joining us today? We will deal with your tardiness later."

Robin guessed this was the headmaster. Kind of like a principal. Which meant she had to do what he said. She'd taken too long making up her mind and had lost her chance. She gathered her backpack and followed him up the steps.

He squinted at her. "We will also need to address your . . . hmm . . . outfit. Unis are not optional, young lady." He stared down at her, his eyes demanding a response.

Again with the uni! Robin decided to echo Mr. Walker, in the hope his response made sense. "Unis are for sheep."

By the way the headmaster puckered his lips, Robin guessed she'd said the wrong thing. She cast her eyes down and meekly followed him into the building.

The school was surprisingly sterile, like a hospital, with white walls and a hard linoleum floor. The headmaster stopped at the end of the hall and pushed on one of the doors, holding it open for her. Robin noted the sign on the doorway: YEAR SIX. As in sixth grade? She was only supposed to be starting sixth grade in the fall. Was Fiona a whole grade ahead of her at school?

The year six class stared at Fiona Walker while Robin stared back.

The first thing she noticed was that everyone was dressed in navy blazers, white shirts, and neckties—even the girls. As in—uniforms. Or unis, for short. Oops. Robin looked down dolefully at her T-shirt, jeans, and sneakers, and pulled her backpack in front of her, just as her cell phone went off.

MNGNG OUTFIT, FI. SHLA

Minging? What did that mean? She guessed nothing good, but she was getting tired of her vocabulary lessons. She glanced around the room and saw a petite, blonde girl smirking at her. Sheila.

A dry-and-airy voice interrupted her thoughts. "Miss Walker, unless there are more calls you need to return, please take your seat."

Robin startled, suddenly realizing "Miss Walker" meant her and followed the voice back to a heavyset, older woman with roller-curled blonde hair, a pink suit, and hard eyes, standing in front of the class. Robin guessed she should do as she was told, but that suddenly seemed too hard. Were their seats assigned, or could she sit anywhere? She hesitated. The teacher's voice grew impatient. "Miss Walker, sit now, please. We have the Eleven Plus coming up and we have a lot of ground to cover."

An impossibly short boy with pointy hair and glasses subtly tapped the seat next to him and gave Robin a tight smile. Robin did her best to thank him with her eyes and slid into the desk.

Instantly, a foot kicked her chair lightly from behind. Robin whipped around, prepared to argue, but balked when she saw her torturer: jet-black curly hair, deep blue eyes, a devilish grin planted on his perfect teeth. Whoa! This guy was paying attention to her? She grinned back, flushed with embarrassment.

"Right. Now. We'll be moving on to maths. Please get out your books...."

Robin forced herself to put the handsome boy out of her mind. She'd already drawn attention from the headmaster and the teacher. If she screwed up again, she'd probably learn the British word for detention.

At midday, the Year Six class filed out of Mrs. Peach's classroom and into the hall. Robin sidled up to the girl named Sheila and whispered, "Where are we going?"

Sheila scrunched up her face. "Fi! Did someone drop you on your head? First that outfit, and now you don't know the schedule. You're positively daft today. We're going to dinner."

"Oh, right," Robin answered, more confused and embarrassed than ever. Dinner? Wasn't it a little early for dinner? But Robin decided not to ask, and she deliberately slowed her pace, not wanting to make any more mistakes in front of Sheila.

Filing through wide double doors, Robin found herself in a cafeteria lunch line. *Dinner*, she realized, was apparently the British word for lunch. Good thing, too, as Robin was absolutely starving. She moved eagerly to the front of the line. A hassled, elderly lunch lady in a hairnet looked up at her.

"Toad-in-a-hole, or ploughman's?" she asked Robin.

Robin looked at her blankly for a moment, her stomach rolling. Toad? British people ate toads? She was still recovering from the jellied eel she'd eaten the day before.

"Um…ploughman's, I guess." She had no idea what a ploughman's was, but it had to be better than toad.

The lunch lady reached behind her and said, "Oh, sorry. All out of ploughman's. Toad-in-a-hole it is," as she indifferently dumped a plate on Robin's tray. Horrified, Robin nearly pushed it back on the counter, but out of forensic curiosity decided to take a peek and see what exactly a cooked toad looked like. Not toad at all—just a browned sausage seated in some kind of pastry. Phew.

She picked up her tray and walked out, looking around the cafeteria, wondering where she should sit. The short boy with glasses lifted his hand. Robin gave him a shy smile and set down her tray at his table.

"Thank you," she said to him. Her cell phone beeped immediately.

WHT RU DNG??!!!

The boy wrinkled his nose. "Here we go. Your friends are going to tell you that you're roughing it."

Roughing it? What did that mean? Robin pulled up her shoulders boldly. "What friends?"

The boy smiled. "That's what I'm always asking YOU, Fi."

A hand tapped impatiently on her shoulder, and Robin turned. Sheila stood directly behind her. "Tony, I need to borrow Fi here for a tick, hope you don't mind." She pinched her fingers on Robin's shoulder—hard—leading her a few steps away from the table.

"What're you doing?" Sheila said. "Rupert's really upset. First you sit next to that tosser in class, now you're having lunch with him?" She gestured flamboyantly at Tony, who shifted his eyes and stared at the table.

Oops—the boyfriend! She'd screwed up again. Fiona had a boyfriend, and he was offended she'd opted to sit with another boy. "I was just . . ." Just what? She was Fiona. She needed to do what Fiona did. "Sorry. Not myself today. Let's go." Robin raced back to Tony's table, apologetic. "I'm sorry about this, I have to go." He nodded in resignation while Robin picked up her tray and wobbled after Sheila. She was stunned when Sheila sat down next to the gorgeous boy from class. The only other empty seat at the table was on his left. Fiona's boyfriend??? No, couldn't be . . .

Robin smiled shyly. "Hi . . . Rupert?"

He grinned at her, the same way he'd done in class. "Are you angry with me, Fi?"

She smiled back. "No. I'm just not myself today." She set her tray down proudly, glowing at the opportunity to claim this boy as her own. Rupert nodded and returned to his conversation with Dave, a thick-necked boy from their class. Rupert didn't speak to Robin again the entire lunch and that was just fine by her, considering how many mistakes she'd already made. Ten minutes later, Rupert spotted the short boy with glasses—Tony—dumping his lunch in the trash. He called out, "You there!"

Tony turned, but kept his eyes low.

Rupert smiled as if he intended to be friendly, but his voice was hard. "Find your own bird, all right?"

Bird? Did bird mean girlfriend?

Tony looked briefly at Robin. Confused and embarrassed, Robin didn't know what to say. She should say something in Tony's defense, but Rupert was Fiona's boyfriend, even if he was being a jerk. And, Robin reasoned, since she didn't plan on being in Fiona's body for long, she probably shouldn't be the reason why Fiona didn't have a boyfriend when she got home. She turned away from Tony and stared at the floor. Out of the corner of her eye, she could see Tony nod and walk off.

"Guess someone fancies YOU, Fi!" Sheila laughed, and everyone joined in. Everyone except Robin.

When school let out, Rupert, Sheila, and Dave quickly claimed Robin at the bus stop. She readily joined them, since she didn't have the faintest idea how to get back to the Walkers' house.

A huge red double-decker bus rounded the corner and Robin could barely suppress her excitement. Two-story buses! In London! She'd only ever seen one, and it was planted like a flowerpot outside a car dealership in Concord, North Carolina. She'd pointed it out to her mom many times, wishing someone would drive it.

The bus screeched to a halt, and Rupert and Sheila stepped aboard, flashing red plastic passes at the driver.

Robin rifled in Fiona's purse, relieved to find a bus pass just like theirs. She flashed it and ran up the stairs to the top deck of the bus.

"Fi!" Sheila called. Robin could hear them all muttering, "Where's she going?"

Robin eagerly claimed a seat in the front row, directly over the head of the bus driver. Rupert, Dave, and Sheila stomped up the stairs after her, giggling. "Are we bloody tourists now?" Sheila teased.

Robin smiled shyly as Rupert sat down beside her but said nothing.

Sheila and Dave quickly launched into a conversation about the Eleven Plus, leaving Robin free to look out the window. She had no intention of being Fiona long enough to worry about whatever the Eleven Plus was. She wanted to see London, from the best possible view. She admired the church spires and gargoyles—real gargoyles! She gasped aloud when she saw a sign that read BAKER STREET, the famed home of Sherlock Holmes. Her dad loved the famous detective and quoted him regularly.

Thoughts of her dad and detective work reminded Robin of her situation. She had to get in touch with Alia! And find out Fiona's birthday. Why in the world did Alia need that? Why was Alia contacting her at all? Robin kept her eyes peeled for the Walkers' house, desperate to get online. She had to find out exactly *what* Alia knew.

chapter five

The Wisher Network

ROBIN GAVE THE DESK DRAWERS ONE LAST good rummage: she couldn't find a single piece of paper that listed Fiona's birthday. She made a brief attempt at the front hall table, but accidentally tipped the huge pile of mail. It all went tumbling to the floor. Frustrated, she hustled upstairs to Fiona's room. Who knew? Maybe Fiona had a diary. Boy, that would help!

Twenty minutes later, Robin found a box of photographs under Fiona's bed. She was rifling through it, checking the date stamps on any that looked like a birthday party, when Mrs. Walker's voice interrupted her.

"Fiona Walker, what ARE you doing?!!!"

Oops. Robin surveyed the mess she'd made. Boxes and papers were everywhere, and Mrs. Walker had an angry look on her face. Robin blurted out, "How many more days until my birthday?"

Mrs. Walker's eyes furrowed. "What?"

"How many more days until my birthday?"

"Days? Try months! Lots of them! Just enough to clean up this mess. Maybe."

"But how many, *exactly*?"

Mrs. Walker paused with a huge sigh, obviously impatient but mentally calculating the answer nevertheless.

Robin suppressed her glee. Sophie asked her mother this question every other day! And like Sophie, all Robin had to do was keep pressing, exhausting Mrs. Walker with the question until she answered.

"Eight months, I suppose. Why? What does that have to do with the state of your room?"

Robin counted eight months from July . . . March. Was the month enough, or did Alia need the exact date? "Is it on a Saturday? I want my party on my *real* birthday, and I can't find my calendar."

"You turned over your room for a—" Mrs. Walker stopped herself and placed a hand on her hip. "Look, Fi, I'll check about the Saturday thing downstairs. I just want to say it's bad enough you cut up all those photos without asking and plastered them on your wall. I let it go because what you made was beautiful. But now you've gone and painted over it. I wish you'd let me know before you do these things. I wanted to keep those pictures."

Oh. Mrs. Walker thought *she'd* painted over the photo border. As if! Robin was about to accuse Jo, but the words stuck in her throat. If she accused the older girl, Mrs. Walker would want the details. Robin would end up steering the conversation away from the birthday information she needed. Sucking in her annoyance, she mumbled, "Sorry."

"Hmph! Just get this cleaned up!"

Robin did as she was told, picking up all of Fiona's things and stuffing them in the closet. Mrs. Walker's voice carried up the stairs five minutes later. "The fourteenth is on a Saturday next year."

"March? You're sure you're looking at March?" Robin called, grinning.

"For God's sake, yes! Yes! March fourteenth, your twelfth birthday, is the second Saturday of the month. So you can stop worrying! Now, is that room straight?"

"Yes ma'am!" Robin cheerfully called out and headed downstairs to the computer. It was already five o'clock—she'd lost a lot of time. If Alia had to work at the pool today, she'd already be gone.

Robin opened Facebook, her fingers trembling as she sent a message to Alia. Within moments, a small chat window appeared in the corner of the screen.

Hello, Wisher. Neera's here 2.

Alia!

SPILL. HOW DID U KNOW?

Went 2 the pool.

Neera couldn't swim. Robin grimaced, imagining how frustrating it must've been for Neera to hang out at the pool, pretending to know Robin's friends, as well as pretending she knew how to swim when she didn't. Alia kept typing.

I guessed she wasn't u.

HOW?

I'll get 2 that. The FB idea is beast, BTW. Yr family doesn't know. I haven't even told Aaron.

Relief flooded Robin. Her family didn't know, so they weren't panicked. At the same time, some part of her wanted them to be panicked. How could they not realize she was missing? Was she so ordinary that anyone could be Robin Haggersly? Robin firmly put her hurt feelings aside. She was here for information. She didn't know how long Alia had to chat.

R u okay? Is the family nice?

THE WALKERS ARE VERY NICE. I'M FINE.

Did u find out Fiona's bday?

Robin responded. MARCH 14 NEXT YEAR IS HER 12TH BDAY.

Great! Plenty of time.

WHAT DO U MEAN?

I'll get to that.

Now Robin was getting irritated. Why was Alia stalling?

DO YOU KNOW WHY THIS HAPPENED?

Ur 11 and you wished. Neera wished at same time 2.

SO?

Any 11-yr-old girl can wish 2 be somebody else. Nothing happens if ur the only one wishing. But if u wish at same time as another 11-year-old girl, you switch bodies and become Wishers. There r many of u all over the world.

SO WHY IS NEERA IN MY BODY AND I'M IN FIONA'S?

Because Fiona was wishing 2.

SO IS FIONA IN NEERA'S BODY, THEN?

Maybe. Might be more.

Anxiety flooded Robin. She typed again. OKAY, SO CAN NEERA AND I WISH OURSELVES BACK? RIGHT NOW?

The response was instant. Wait.

Wait? That was the last thing Robin wanted to do.

U JUST SAID WISHERS GET INTO ANOTHER GIRL'S BODY BY WISHING—

Alia's message pinged in the corner of the screen before Robin could even finish.

If u and Neera wish now, u might get back, but Neera probably won't. Unlikely Fiona—or whoever's in Neera's body—will be wishing right now.

HOW DO YOU—

She'd go into the body of another Wisher. Maybe Fiona. Maybe smbdy else. Depends who's wishing— some girls change bodies many x. Best 2 wait & wish when u've found all Wishers in ur network. Less risk. Probably just Fiona left 2 find.

—KNOW ALL OF THIS?

No sudden ping this time. Robin shifted, impatient

71

for the answer. When Alia's response finally arrived, Robin's eyes widened in surprise.

Because I was one.

YOU WERE A WISHER?!!!

Y.

HOW DID U GET HOME THEN?

Alia's pause was so long Robin checked her Internet connection.

Wished. Not sure of details—wasn't in charge. Just told when 2 wish. I should've asked mre questions but I didn't. I will help u guys find Fiona. Might take few days.

Robin frowned, wondering whether Alia was telling everything she knew. Plus, the idea of waiting, when she was pretty sure she could get home right now, wasn't tempting. The computer pinged again.

Robin—its Neera here now—I won't make u wait. We can wish now and if it works, at least u will get home.

Robin's throat clogged. Neera had to be the bravest girl she'd ever met. Alia had just told them wishing was risky, even when you planned it, so it was best to wait until all the Wishers in your network had been found. And despite that, Neera was offering to wish right now, not knowing where she would go, just so Robin, a girl she barely knew, could go home. Surely Robin could find the strength to be Fiona for a few more days. She typed quickly and sent the message before she could change her mind.

NO WAY, NEERA. I WON'T LEAVE U.

U sure????

SURE, I'M SURE. WHAT WE NEED IS A PLAN 2 FIND FIONA. NEERA, U SAID U DON'T HAVE A PHONE OR INTERNET. CAN YOU SEND SNAIL MAIL? IF IT'S ADDRESSED TO U, WILL U GET IT?

Yes! I can do that. What should I say?

TELL FIONA 2 GET IN TOUCH. TELL HER WHERE THERE'S A COMPUTER, OR A PHONE.

I'll send 2day.

OKAY, BUT LOOKING 4 FIONA ISN'T ENOUGH. CAN U PUT ALIA BACK ON?

After a short pause, Alia was back.

Y?

ALIA, U SAID FIONA MIGHT NOT BE IN NEERA'S BODY?

Probably, but not definitely.

SO WE NEED TO FIND AS MANY WISHERS AS WE CAN, JUST IN CASE. WE HAVE 2 GET THEM 2 THE FB PAGE—CAN'T WAIT 4 THEM 2 FIND US. ANYWAY, JUST TALKING TO MRE WISHERS WILL GIVE US MRE INFO.

Agreed. How do we find them?

Robin paused, trying to remember all the dull programming lessons her Web-designing mom had given her. When the idea hit, Robin couldn't believe she hadn't thought of doing it before. She typed a single-word answer—KEYWORDS.

What do u mean?

Mrs. Walker's voice rang out from the kitchen. "Fi! Teatime!"

"'Kay!" Robin responded. Why were English people always drinking tea? Oh, well. If Mrs. Walker was anything like her own mother, Robin had a few more minutes. She typed faster.

SAY U WANTED TO BUY FRIZZ EASE. ONLY U DON'T REMEMBER THE NAME. U JUST KNOW IT'S A SPECIAL SHAMPOO FOR FRIZZY HAIR. SO YOU SEARCH FOR "FRIZZY," "HAIR," AND "SHAMPOO." FRIZZ EASE POPS UP ON PAGE 1 OF YOUR SEARCH INSTEAD OF PAGE 20, BECAUSE THE WEB DESIGNER CHECKED OUT WHICH KEYWORDS CUSTOMERS USE THE MOST WHEN THEY SEARCH. SO IF WE DO A KEYWORD SEARCH FOR "WISHING," WE COULD ADD THOSE WORDS 2 OUR PAGE, SO OTHER WISHERS FIND US FASTER. I'LL DO THE SEARCH RIGHT NOW. ALIA, CAN U ADD THEM, 'CAUSE I HAVE 2 GO IN A MINUTE?

Robin zinged over to Google and typed in *Wishers*. The results made her gasp. She sent them to Neera and Alia without comment. For a few minutes, no one typed anything. The most common keywords used for "Wishing" were: *birthday, magic, change, eleven,* and *girl.*

Keywords did not become keywords by chance. Robin knew that from her mom. They were the words people used most often when they searched. So when

Alia had said, "There are a lot of you," and meant there are a lot of Wishers, she wasn't kidding. Lots of people made wishes. Heck, Robin couldn't even count the number of times she'd said "I wish" in her life, let alone how many times she'd heard someone else say it. And that wasn't even including Christmases and birthdays! But of the people in the world who were searching online for their wishes to come true, the most frequent searchers were eleven-year-old girls. Girls who suddenly found themselves in another body, in another country with no idea how to get home. They were out there, somewhere, just as lost as Robin and Neera.

Neera finally made a comment.

I think this is bigger than just u and me.

"Me too," Robin whispered.

Tea, Robin discovered as she walked in the kitchen, did not include tea. It was the British word for dinner, just as dinner had been British for lunch. Jo was already at the table, as Mrs. Walker placed something as mysterious as toad-in-the-hole on Robin's plate.

"What're we having?" Robin asked dolefully.

Jo scrunched up her face. "What's it look like? Bubble and squeak."

Robin nodded to cover her mistake, but she was instantly intrigued. Bubble and squeak? Sounded like candy. Encouraged, she took a huge first bite and gagged into her napkin. Not candy! Cabbage. And ground beef. Not bad, just ... unexpected.

Mrs. Walker sat down and turned to Robin. "Talked to your dad. New lighting designer is working out brilliantly. You'll be back at rehearsals tomorrow."

Robin stared at her blankly, her mouth full of food, while Jo snorted, and muttered, "Lighting designer! Dad's just stalling—"

Mrs. Walker placed a hand over Jolene's to shush her. She gave her younger daughter a sympathetic look, apparently mistaking Robin's confusion for panic. "It's all right, darling, you'll be great. I was just saying your dad found a new lighting designer. He's staying late to do a tech run tonight, and you can start rehearsals again tomorrow, all fresh."

The play! She'd forgotten all about it! Fiona was supposed to play a part in some play! Robin's stomach churned. Above and beyond the fact she didn't know the lines or the part or even the play, she'd never been onstage. In fact, the only time she'd ever had people watching her was at swim meets—and look how that had turned out! No, she couldn't do it. Maybe she could say she was losing her voice. She'd just have to hope that her plan to find Fiona worked—quickly. How long did it take for a letter to get to India anyway?

Jolene scowled and kicked her under the table. A muffled "Ow!" escaped Robin's mouth.

"Jo!" Mrs. Walker said harshly.

"Sorry, she's just not even here," Jolene said, a whine in her voice.

"She's got a lot on her mind. The play, the Eleven Plus. Leave her alone."

That Eleven Plus thing again! The name made it sound like a day-care center, but she guessed it wasn't. Whatever it was, it was definitely important. Even though she was hungry, Robin had a hard time swallowing. Jolene was right—Fiona wasn't here. But she needed to be, to avert impending disaster.

After tea, Robin raced back to the computer, opened the Facebook page, and smiled. Alia had added all the keywords to their page. Neera popped up in the chat room.

Do you like it?

LOVE IT.

Another thought struck Robin.

IS ALIA STILL THERE?

No. Gone 2 pool.

Robin fretted for a minute and finally typed.

WHY DID ALIA DEMAND I FIND FIONA'S BDAY? FORGOT 2 ASK.

Don't know. She asked me same thing about my birthday. Maybe she just wanted to make sure we were 11. That we really are Wishers.

MAYBE, Robin typed. But the question nagged at her. Neera was already switching subjects.

Robin, who are "The Birds"?

The term made Robin instantly homesick.

NICKNAME. ME AND BFF WRENN—ROBIN AND WRENN, BOTH BIRDS.

Do u mind if I go 2 her house tomorrow? She invited me.

Robin felt an ugly tickle in her stomach. It was hard enough to share her family—she hadn't really planned on sharing her best friend. But Neera was supposed to be Robin, and if she refused, Wrenn would think she was mad at her. Reluctantly, she typed.

GO. IT'S COOL.

I have a confession.

"Runt!" Jolene stood in the doorway. "You've been on the computer all afternoon. I got me O Levels this week!"

"'Kay, just a sec!" Robin said. Jo folded her arms and tapped her foot. Robin stalled by asking, "Uhhh. . . what're O Levels?" while she read Neera's message.

I let your mom cut my hair. I'm sorry if that makes u mad—it just itched like crazy!

The head lice. Without thinking, Robin touched her hair—Fiona's—hair. The sensation was completely unfamiliar—Fiona's hair was thinner and surprisingly rough. While Robin's hair had always been a pain to brush because it was so thick, it was always soft and silky to the touch. The difference only made Robin feel worse. Saturday night, it had been vitally important that she kept her long hair, even if it meant submitting to that horrible metal comb until her mom was satisfied all the lice were gone. Now, Robin wouldn't care if she were bald, if it meant she could be Robin again. Neera misunderstood her silence.

R u angry? I can send you a picture, if you like.

Robin contemplated the offer, trying to imagine looking at a picture of herself that she'd never sat for. The idea terrified her, although she didn't know why.

Jolene exploded. "You know bloody well what O Levels are—my exams! Same as your Eleven Plus, which you're supposed to be studying for! So leave off!"

Robin typed hurriedly.

NOT ANGRY. IT'S OKAY. BUT NO PICS, THX. GOTTA GO.

As Jo reached for the mouse, Robin quickly switched the computer off, just to make sure she didn't see the Facebook page. Jo looked ready to strangle her. "Oh, bloody great! What'd you do that for? Now I have to reboot! MUM!"

Upstairs, Robin lay down on Fiona's bed and picked up the copy of *Peter Pan* on the bedside table. She read Wendy's lines at a whisper, not wanting anyone to hear her lame attempts at acting. She might look like Fiona, but she wasn't beautiful, smart, popular, or talented like Fiona. Just boring, ordinary Robin Haggersly. If she had to play Wendy, she'd mess up, and the entire audience would know just how un-special Robin was.

She drifted off to sleep, lights on, the play across her chest. She woke a mere hour later, shaking from a nightmare in which she was a fully grown Fiona Walker, greeting an eleven-year-old Robin Haggersly as a stranger.

Bleary-eyed on Tuesday morning, Robin located Fiona's uniform in her closet and pulled it on. She was determined to get the school thing right. At least now she *looked* like the other students. She waited for the bus outside the Walker house and proudly flipped her bus pass at the driver. She was making her first solo trip on a bus—and in London, no less!

Tony was absent from school. She wouldn't be able to apologize to him today. She focused on the positive—she could enjoy Rupert's attention all day long without guilt. Her schoolwork was a little more worrying. When the teacher handed back the writing assignment she'd done the day before, there was a big red *D* and a *See Me* notation at the top.

As the rest of the class filed to the dining hall for lunch, *no*, dinner, Robin wandered up to the teacher's desk, paper in hand. Mrs. Peach barely even looked up as she growled, "Miss Walker, have you perchance been perusing an *American* dictionary at home?"

Robin suddenly felt naked. "I'm not sure. Why?"

"Because all your words are spelled like an American's. How do you spell *color*, for example?"

Easy. Robin lifted her shoulders with pride. "C-O-L-O-R."

Mrs. Peach pursed her lips and smiled, as though she'd cleverly found the secret to Robin's stupidity. "That would be how an American spells it. We are English. The word is spelled C-O-L-O-*U*-R," she said, emphasizing the *U* like Robin was in first grade. "I take a point off for every spelling error, so see that you use a proper dictionary from now on."

In the dining hall, Rupert waved her over. Robin set her tray on the table. Today's supper—"Bangers and mash"—sounded weird, but turned out to be a sausage and mashed potatoes

"What'd Fuzzy want?" Sheila demanded.

Fuzzy? Oh, wait. Mrs. Peach—Fuzzy. Peaches are fuzzy. Robin grinned at the nickname and shrugged. "She gave me a bad grade, just because I used an American dictionary. I mean, it's not wrong, technically. . . ."

"Neither are your table manners!" Dave declared. Sheila laughed out loud. Even Rupert smothered a giggle. Robin flushed. What was wrong with her table manners? She looked quickly at her tray—napkin, knife, fork, no splatter or spillage on the uni—what was wrong? Was she chewing with her mouth open?

Rupert gently explained, "Your knife and fork. We were wondering why you hold them like an American all of a sudden."

Robin glanced around and realized everyone was eating with a knife in their left hand, fork in the right. Everyone except her. Could she do it that way? She doubted it—not without practice. To cover, she flipped her hair and looked at Dave. "Just felt like it," she told him defiantly. To make her point, she skewered a piece of lettuce and stuffed it in her mouth. Rupert grinned. He switched his silverware around and followed suit.

"Lemme try!" Sheila squealed.

After school, Mrs. Walker greeted her with a change of clothes. "Your father's on his way to get you—rehearsal starts in an hour. Here. Have a change and wash until he gets here. Be sure to bring your books with you. You can revise backstage between scenes."

Revise? What did revise mean? Robin's interest in translating faded as the words *rehearsal starts in an hour* registered. The play! Robin panicked. She hadn't studied the lines. She'd meant to, she'd even brought the script to school. But her mind had wandered with Rupert's attentions. She needed to get out of this! She made a small cough and said in a raspy voice, "I don't think I'm feeling well."

Mrs. Walker didn't even pause. "None of that now, darling. You've played the invalid for too many rehearsals. You need the practice, and the show must go on." She nodded at the front door. "Here's Dad. Go change now, quickly."

Robin felt like a kid who hadn't done her final project for school. Only this was much, much, worse. She was doomed.

chapter six

Dori Simpson of Honolulu, Hawaii

AS NERVOUS AS ROBIN FELT ABOUT THE dreaded rehearsal, her eyes grew wide as she spotted Big Ben from the car window. She really was in London! The famous clock looked beautiful, glowing like a Christmas tree with lights all the way up the tall, sandstone-colored façade. Then Big Ben disappeared under the glow of a major intersection, with cars dashing around in happy chaos. Up above were neon signs—millions of them—blinking and flashing dizzying colors and images as they advertised plays like *Rent* and *Hamlet*.

Mr. Walker zipped around a corner and parked. Robin climbed out of the car and gawked at the lights and the people . . . thousands of them . . . hustling across the many intersecting streets. Mr. Walker was smiling as he joined her. "Looking for something, my darling?"

"Where ARE we?" Robin asked.

Surprised, he wrinkled his nose. "Piccadilly Circus. Where did you think we were?" He snorted. "Here, let me show you something." He covered her eyes and turned her around. "Now open and look up."

Robin craned her neck and stared in disbelief. The theater was gigantic! It was bigger than a church, bigger than the auditorium in downtown Raleigh. Its four soaring columns didn't even reach the roof—there were two more stories above them!

Suddenly, a billboard between the columns fizzed. Bits of color assembled and reassembled themselves, like pieces of a puzzle put together by invisible hands. A smiling Fiona Walker appeared, in an old-fashioned, blue-and-white, high-necked dress, on the arm of a laughing Peter Pan. *PETER PAN*: STARRING LIAM RUTHERFORD & INTRODUCING FIONA WALKER flashed the sign. The image broke apart and reassembled again. FIRST THREE WEEKS SOLD OUT! CALL FOR TICKETS NOW!

Robin gasped. She recognized Peter Pan—she'd seen him in a couple of films on the Disney Channel. She was starring in a play with *him*? Mr. Walker regarded her tenderly as he steered her across the sidewalk to the theater entrance. "Like it, darling? I thought you might. Now come on, my young starlet, let's get to rehearsal." He opened the door with a sweeping gesture. "After you, milady."

Robin's mouth was still hanging open as she followed Mr. Walker inside. A grand foyer with crystal chandeliers gave way to a gigantic auditorium that had to seat thousands. Looking upward, she spotted two balconies—and loads of real balcony boxes! She gasped again. No way could she make an idiot of herself in front of this many people. She'd never had the courage to even try out for the community theater around the corner from her home. Now she was STARRING IN LONDON? In a real play with a movie star?

She looked at the stage and saw a gigantic brass bed and an enormous antique wardrobe. A window next to the bed twinkled with lights, showing a glowing backdrop of nighttime London. Men wearing headsets and carrying toolboxes hustled back and forth, shouting as they wielded hammers and drills.

A woman with a clipboard cackled orders. At the sight of Robin, she said, "Ah! Look who's here!" Robin thought she sounded nice, but the disappointed expression on her face suggested she wasn't as pleased to see Fiona as she claimed. Mr. Walker's lips were tight as he answered, "Course, she's bloody here. Told you she would be."

"OI! YOU!" A young woman with a spiky pink Mohawk pointed at Robin and waggled her finger. Robin had never seen anyone like her in all of North Carolina. She looked positively alien, with about a million earrings puncturing her ears, nose, and lips. Plus, she wore a hot-pink miniskirt and boots. "You're late. I'll have to do your hair with a curling iron as it is. No time for rollers."

Mr. Walker smiled at Robin. "Backstage you go,

princess. Hair and makeup, right now. Follow Stef."
Robin did as instructed, but she heard Mr. Walker hiss
quietly at the woman with the clipboard, "Give her a
chance, would you?!".

Robin picked her way up the steps to the stage
and followed the fast-moving Stef to a dressing room.
While Robin was ogling the room, Stef handed her
the blue-and-white dress she'd seen on the billboard
and ordered, "Get your togs off and get dressed. Don't
forget the tights!"

Togs? Robin guessed that meant clothes. She did
as she was told—Stef was frankly too scary-looking
to argue with—and followed her down the hall to the
makeup room. Five sets of eyebrows lifted in surprise
when Robin walked in. Two were makeup artists, the
rest were actors: two boys even younger than Robin,
whom she assumed played Wendy's brothers, and
a man dressed as Captain Hook. The actors were
sheathed in plastic up to their necks and absolutely
globbed with heavy foundation makeup and eyeliner.
Captain Hook seemed familiar—like Robin had seen
him in a movie, too—but he looked pretty weird with
all the makeup.

"Ah. So young Miss Walker is joining us again,
then?" Hook smirked knowingly at the makeup artists.
They shot him looks of sympathy.

The younger boy piped up, "Wasn't sure you were
coming back, Fi."

Robin had no idea what was going on. Why did everyone seem so surprised that Fiona was here? Didn't they know her face was plastered on a billboard outside? She decided to play it cool. "I wasn't sure I'd be here, either."

An hour and a half later, Robin stared at herself in the mirror: hair and makeup complete, beautiful Fiona had been transformed into stunning Wendy. The wire from the microphone scratched at her chest, and the heavy metal cable lashed to her back was extremely uncomfortable, but she was onstage! In London! A star!

Stagehands led Robin and the actors who played her brothers onstage to the giant brass bed as they guided the metal cables from above. Robin was last onto the bed, with easy access to center stage—Wendy would be the first to get up when Peter cried over his lost shadow. Robin shut her eyes tight, trying to remember her lines. In the first scenes, they were all "Who are you?" "Why?" "How?" She'd memorized them while she sat in hair and makeup, but she had no idea what her lines were after that. She prayed there would be a break in between scenes, so she could look them up.

The stage went dark. Then suddenly, music! A whole orchestra, playing the familiar overture! Robin fidgeted under the bedcovers, excited. Who would have ever dreamed she'd be here, in London, starring onstage? This was a *million* times better than being Robin Haggersly! She was going to be *great*. A star!

The lights came up slowly. She slammed her eyes shut, as a xylophone played. The youngest boy—who Robin had learned was playing John—nudged her and whispered, "Here comes Tinkerbell."

Robin realized she hadn't seen anyone who looked remotely like Tinkerbell backstage—she'd have wings, wouldn't she? But no one did. What did she look like? Robin deliberated taking a peek. No, best to wait.

The movie star actor playing Peter Pan entered through the window and delivered his opening line: "Hello, there, Tink. Have you found him, then?" Robin couldn't resist taking a quick peek at Peter through the covers. He was much shorter than he looked onscreen, but his smile was wide and his blond hair peered out from under the green cap. Definitely him. Robin sucked in a breath, scarcely able to believe she'd be sharing the stage with him in just a minute. She pulled the cover over her head as she heard a clatter and he spoke the next line, "Aha! There you are, shadow!" More clatter. Her moment was coming up. She was so excited she could barely breathe. The closet doors opened and slammed shut again. Toys fell to the stage floor. Peter Pan tried to catch his shadow and finally gave up. When Robin heard him cry, she leapt out of bed with her line.

"Why are you crying, boy?"

"CUT!" called a voice from the audience. The

other actors made loud, sighing noises and gestures of exasperation. Mr. Walker smiled at her sweetly and said, "Fi, darling, you've just stepped on Tinkerbell."

Robin looked around, seeing no one. Mr. Walker pointed to the floor, where a fluttering white light danced around her feet. Oh. So that was Tinkerbell.

Late that night, Robin was in the car, making a silent, tearful vow she'd never act again. Until now, she'd thought her eleventh birthday was the most humiliating day of her life. But the play rehearsal was even worse. She'd been a disaster—worse than she'd ever imagined she could be—and it wasn't because she didn't know the lines. Those she actually found pretty easy, and she'd quickly learned that whenever she forgot, she could call out "line" and the woman with the clipboard would read it to her. The trouble was her movement. Stepping on Tinkerbell had been only the first of many, many mistakes. When the flying scene came, the cable had lifted her into the air without warning, and she'd screamed. On a second try, she'd lifted perfectly, but in her efforts to "fly" she'd tangled all the cables together, until she, Peter Pan, John, and Michael looked like fish on a line. They'd never even made it to Act Two. All because of her.

Blocking! She'd never heard the term. She supposed it made sense that the actors "blocked a scene"—picked out where they were going to move—long in advance of the actual show. But how was she supposed to know that? Plus, every movement had to be exactly the same, every single time. And she couldn't do it, because she wasn't Fiona Walker, glamorous star, daughter of Mr. Walker, the director. She was stupid, clumsy, ordinary Robin Haggersly from North Carolina, who goofed up everything no matter who she was or where she was.

The worst part of all was that she'd loved it. Every minute she was onstage. She'd dreaded it, and she'd been AWFUL, but she'd never had so much fun in her life. Underneath the lights, the microphone echoing her voice all the way to the third-tier balconies, Robin felt like Wendy must've felt when Peter Pan flew in her window—magical, special, and wonderful. She'd never felt that way before—not from swimming, or piano recitals, not even when she was scoring a goal at soccer. It was the biggest game of pretend she'd ever played and she'd loved digging into her imagination to figure out every movement and reaction she thought a heroine like Wendy would make. She obviously had no talent, but she wanted to do this more than anything she'd ever done.

The other kids—the ones playing her brothers and the Lost Boys—had all been nice about it, like they felt sorry for her, but she could still remember Captain Hook throwing off his hat and shouting, "Unbelievable! Who knew it was possible to cock this up more than she did on Saturday? But she's done it! And—!"

Peter Pan put a hand on Hook's shoulder as he said, "Look, mate, that's enough. Fi's just a girl—"

Hook shrugged him off and continued, "The play opens two weeks from tonight! It's going to be an utter fiasco."

Fiasco? What was a fiasco? She supposed it wasn't anything good. Still, she was grateful to Peter Pan for coming to her rescue.

In the car, Robin turned to face Mr. Walker. "Mr. Walker?" she said quietly. He continued to drive, singing to himself. She cleared her throat and spoke a little louder. "Um, Dad?"

He smiled at her. "Yes, darling?"

"Don't you think it would be better if I quit the play?"

He screeched the car over to the curb and shut off the engine. He looked at her, his soft, gray eyes focused on her face. He really was a very kind man. He'd never lost patience with her, and he'd even shouted over Captain Hook, "I'm the bloody director! And as far as I'm concerned, if any actor in this cast is replaceable, all of you are." Captain Hook was quiet after that, while Mr. Walker patiently took her through the blocking, over and over again.

The worst part was when Mr. Walker called for a break. She was trying to find her way backstage to hide when she heard Peter Pan saying to Hook, "Look, mate, she's his *daughter*," emphasizing the word. "And if he has to pick, well, who do you think he's going to pick?" He hadn't been defending her at all—he'd been trying to save Hook's job.

Tears welled in her eyes just thinking about it.

As late as it was—eleven o'clock by her best guess—there was still enough twilight for Mr. Walker to see her brimming eyes. Robin turned away and Mr. Walker took her hand. "Now look here, Fi. Don't turn away, I want you to see me say this." Robin reluctantly lifted her head. "I don't want you to quit. I'll admit I had my doubts on Saturday, but I saw something tonight. You had a bit of the jitters coming back, but that's all it was, darling. What matters is whether you *want* to do this, or whether you want to quit." He searched her face for an answer.

"I ... I feel like I should," Robin said slowly.

Mr. Walker rushed in. "Never mind what you *should* do. Tell me what you *want* to do."

"But I was horrible!"

"You weren't horrible. Get that out of your head right now." He wrinkled his brow. "Actually, you were better tonight than you've ever been." She rolled her eyes. "No, really, when it came to the acting part, you were brilliant! Darling, my job is on the line here," he insisted. "I wouldn't say that if I didn't mean it. You were a natural. I don't know what happened to you between Saturday and tonight, but it's worth doing.

What do you say? I'm willing to try it if you are." He looked at her again. "Do you want to try?"

Wait a second. She was good? Not perfect Fiona Walker—she, Robin Haggersly, was a good actress. This was a professional director telling her she was good! She felt a small ray of hope and croaked out, "More than anything."

He picked up her hand and kissed it. "Then that's all that matters." He gently wiped the tears from her eyes. "There now. I have a plan, but let's get under way, shall we?" He started the car again. "Now, tomorrow. Forget school. We're going back to the theater. We'll go through the blocking until we've got it. Every last lift of a finger."

"And the lines," Robin reminded him. "Pretend I don't know anything."

"Right you are. Fiona Walker is now my brave understudy, taking over a role mere days before opening night. I have to teach her everything from scratch. I'll get our Peter Pan to join us after lunch, and we'll work again, just the three of us...."

Robin was drifting off to sleep in Fiona's bed when she realized she'd forgotten to check Facebook. She tiptoed downstairs. Neither Neera nor Alia was online. The Facebook page was empty, too. No one had found them.

It would be easy to give up and go to bed. She had to be up early in the morning to go back to the theater. But after an evening of failure, she needed success. Finding a Wisher, she decided, would definitely make her feel better.

She opened up Google. Had the keywords even worked? Could a Wisher even find their Facebook page? She'd never checked. Her fingers whizzed across the keyboard: *wishing, birthday, girl, eleven, change*, and *magic*. As the results loaded, Robin realized something. Yes, she'd added the keywords to draw people to her Facebook site. But she'd never used the keywords to see if any other Wisher had used them, too, and built a Web site of their *own*. Curious, she scrolled through the results.

Google listed millions of Web sites that used the words *wishing, birthday, girl, eleven, change*, and *magic*. On about Web site number fifty, Robin found a photograph of a really pretty, blonde, blue-eyed, eleven-year-old girl named Samantha De Groot, with a caption.

HEY! I'M DORI. OR AT LEAST I WAS. UNTIL I MADE A WISH. CHECK OUT HOW I'VE CHANGED!!! MAGIC! TRUST ME, DORI SIMPSON LOOKS NOTHING LIKE THIS, AND I HAVEN'T HAD A MAKEOVER. LOL! ANYWAY, I'M SAMANTHA DE GROOT NOW, I'M 11 AND LIVING IN SOUTH AFRICA. I'M ABSOLUTELY GORGEOUS AND MY PARENTS ARE LOADED. HOW COOL IS THAT??? WONDERING IF ANY OTHER GIRLS HAVE EVER HAD THIS HAPPEN. WRITE BACK IF YOU HAVE. IT WOULD BE FUN TO TALK. WE'D BE LIKE A SECRET CLUB!

"Gotcha," Robin whispered, as she clicked on Samantha's email address.

chapter seven

Being Fiona

STAGE LIGHTS, ROBIN LEARNED THE NEXT morning, are extremely hot. They hadn't bothered her at six a.m. when they started rehearsing. But now it was noon. The building was warm with midday sun, and every time Robin stood under her spotlight, trickles of sweat dripped down her back. Mr. Walker noticed she was withering and apologized. "Air-conditioning's only for the punters, I'm afraid."

Robin looked at him quizzically. "Punters?"

"The audience. Bums on seats, that's what its all about." He adjusted a spotlight. "Now, in this scene, you're on a small island, surrounded by crocodiles. You—Wendy—have no way off, until you spy a kite. The kite is over here, just above the right balcony. It comes down on this cable. . . ." He hit the button on a small remote control. The kite started a steep incline toward the stage.

"Cool! Can I try that?" Robin leaned over, her hand out.

"No," he said calmly. "Unless you can show me

exactly where you're supposed to be standing on your island, in order to see the kite."

Robin jumped and planted her feet. "Here."

Mr. Walker switched on the spotlight. Robin felt the heat of the lamp on her face—she got it right!

A jubilant Mr. Walker called out, "And Bob's your uncle!" Robin opened her eyes and looked around for someone named Bob. Ohhh. No Bob. Just another British phrase. Pleased, she held out her hand for the kite remote control, and Mr. Walker proudly passed it to her.

"Bloody burning up in here. Fancy some water?" Mr. Walker asked.

Robin nodded, intent on moving the kite up and down.

She'd woken at five in the morning and found Mr. Walker in the kitchen, already sipping tea. They'd smiled at each other, accomplices in a prank: they would fool everyone into believing Fiona Walker was a great actress. Or else she'd quit. Robin had insisted on that part of the deal. She couldn't stand bombing out over and over again, making everybody mad. It wasn't fair to her or the cast. Mr. Walker reluctantly agreed. If she failed, the understudy—whoever she might be— would take over the role.

Robin toyed with the idea of deliberately bombing out. After all, she really needed to be online with Neera and Alia, figuring out a way to get home. She did not need to be in a theater with Mr. Walker, learning how to act. But the memory of yesterday was still a fresh wound, on which Mr. Walker's warm encouragement was working like a lotion.

Basically, she couldn't resist trying.

The stage had been freezing cold when they got there. And spooky! Every footstep echoed so loudly that Robin was sure she was making mistakes even when she wasn't. Plus, she felt plain silly pretending Mr. Walker was Peter Pan: calling him "boy," holding his hand as Peter taught Wendy to fly, and running through Neverland together. Some of her mistakes were embarrassing, like not knowing "stage right" was the left of the stage and vice versa. But Mr. Walker waved off her stomping little dances of frustration. By mid-morning the theater had grown warm with summer heat, and Robin had warmed up, too, partly because of the temperature, but mostly from a growing sense of confidence. By noon she and Mr. Walker were congratulating each other.

Mr. Walker returned and handed her a bottle of water. She poured the cold liquid on her sweaty head as he announced, "Just called our Peter, luv. He's on his way."

Robin nodded, sucking back the anxiety she felt about acting with Peter Pan again. It was one thing to perform for Mr. Walker, who believed in her, but something else entirely to perform with someone who thought she was a disaster.

Mr. Walker's cell phone rang, and he grimaced when he saw who was calling. "Your mum. Wait just a tic." He answered the call with a bright "Good morning, my darling," but Robin could hear Mrs. Walker's voice booming through the phone.

"Just got a call from the headmaster! Nigel—"

"Darling, let me explain," Mr. Walker interrupted.

"Fi's final practice exams for the Eleven Plus were today! You promised—"

Mr. Walker smiled at Robin even as he drifted away with the phone, his shoulders slouching a bit in the face of Mrs. Walker's anger. But he remained calm, whispering apologies and soothing words before hanging up a few minutes later. He spotted the worry on Robin's face and wrinkled his nose. "Not to worry, my darling. If anyone's in trouble with Mum, it's me, not you. Now, then."

Mr. Walker disappeared into the "wings"—that was what the sides of the stage behind the curtains were called. "I just want to try one last thing before Peter gets here." He walked out, holding a familiar cable. "Let's get this flying thing down, shall we?"

Robin frowned, remembering how she'd tangled herself up in the cables the night before, and three other actors with her. Mr. Walker saw her pout and pulled her toward him. "You've got to trust me. Do you?"

She nodded with the realization she did trust him. She trusted him like she trusted . . . well, her dad.

He smiled and snapped the belt around her waist, and connected the steel line to her back. "There's a good girl. Come on then, nothing to it. Peter says his line and you try to fly. Trick is, you've got to count after Peter's line. Peter says blah, blah, blah, then count to three. Nice and even. Do it with me. One, two, threeeee!!!"

Mr. Walker launched her into the air. Robin shrieked.

"Bril! Marvelous! That was PERFECT!"

Robin drifted, twenty feet above him. "But I shrieked!" she argued.

"So does Wendy! Wendy's never flown before, either." He adjusted the cable. "That's what made your performance so brilliant! Every line sounded like you were saying it for the first time, exactly how Wendy would be."

Robin's heart sank. Now she understood why Mr. Walker thought she was so great. Fiona had been reciting Wendy's lines in rehearsal for . . . how long? Weeks? Months? Robin didn't know exactly, but she was pretty sure it was a long time. Fiona probably did start to sound a little mechanical, saying the exact same thing that many times. Meanwhile, Robin *was* saying them for the first time. What if it turned out she was no good?

"Now then, darling. Let's plot your flight. From the top of the wardrobe, count three. Then you land on the bed, pet Nana, count five, and off stage left. Got it?"

"Right." Robin flew, landed, counted, and recited her lines. She bounced from spot to spot, unenthusiastic.

Mr. Walker grabbed the cable, causing her to dangle in midair. "All of a sudden, you sound like you're reading. What's wrong?"

"Nothing's wrong. It's just that . . ." She pondered how to ask. "Pretend last night was different. That I was an understudy, and I was reading the lines for the first time. What if I'm no good tonight, because I know the lines?"

He sighed. "Fi, children are either natural actors or they're not. Those that play pretend games, like you did not so long ago, can act on any professional stage in the world. All they need is confidence, which I hope I'm giving you today. And a sense of fun." He pursed his lips and looked at her again. "Maybe that's what we need. We've been working for hours. Let's have some fun!" Mr. Walker eagerly pulled on the fly cables again, launching her back into the air. "I want to see you FLY." And with that, he pushed on her feet—hard—sending her vaulting toward the rafters.

She screamed out "AHHH!!!" but there was a smile on her face. He started laughing as Robin swung back in the opposite direction, like a pendulum. He laughed so hard he got the hiccups, which sent them both into fits.

"Now, Wendy!" *Hic.* "Bugger. Say your line!" he barked.

She screamed joyfully, "I'M FLYING!!!"

"Now we're talking!" They both dissolved into laughter.

Robin felt positively triumphant when they pulled outside the Walker home at midnight. True, she'd flubbed things a bit when Peter arrived. But he'd flashed her a dizzying smile and she'd forgotten about his doubts and started acting. After the exhausting day of training, they'd done a full dress rehearsal with the entire cast. Robin still made mistakes, but none on par with the fiasco she'd caused the night before. As they'd gathered for "notes"—Mr. Walker's comments on the performance—Stef had started a round of applause as Robin came onstage. The rest of the cast and crew joined in.

Robin shyly accused them, "You're just applauding because I didn't mess up."

Peter pointed out, "Reason enough, Miss Walker. And anyway, we actors never argue with applause."

Robin still felt a shiver when she thought of his words—*we actors*—meaning she was included in their number.

"Now then, may we get on with notes?" Mr. Walker asked effusively. "First, Bob!" The director gave the actor who played the pirate captain a stern look. "Where was your bloody hook for Act Five?"

Hook threw up his hands. "I honestly don't know! I set it on the prop table, I'm sure of it!"

. . .

At home, Mr. Walker started to regale Mrs. Walker with stories of Fiona's triumph, but she simply turned on Robin and said, "Bed. School tomorrow, no excuses."

Robin nodded and submitted to the order willingly, more tired than she'd ever been in her life. Mr. Walker started to protest, but Mrs. Walker shot a dark look at him. Robin knew the look—her own mother occasionally cast one at Robin's dad when they disagreed. And, like her own dad, Mr. Walker hushed up.

For the first time since she'd been in England, Robin dreamed a happy dream. She was a grown Fiona Walker again, but this time she was receiving an award, amid the flashes of a thousand cameras and thunderous applause.

At school the next day, a bleary-eyed Robin tried to pay attention, but she was too tired to even remember her teacher's name. All she could think was "Fuzzy" as the teacher droned on and on about the importance of the looming Eleven Plus exam.

"Soon, your primary school education here at Clarendon will be over. Many of you who pass the Eleven Plus will have the option of grammar school, college, and, eventually, university. Those who don't pass will attend the local technical school."

Robin wondered why Fuzzy made no forecast for what happened *after* technical school. She made it sound permanent, like jail. Robin raised her hand. "Sorry, Mrs . . . ," she started. In her few days in England, she'd learned it was best to start any question with the word "sorry." She had no idea why, but the British seemed to like the word, and Robin wanted to be liked. But what was the teacher's NAME? "Uh, what *is* technical school?"

"S'where you learn how to top off the oil on the car!" Rupert joked. Dave snorted.

"Mr. Sellars!" Fuzzy said sharply before addressing Robin. "There are many fine careers to be had after attending technical school, Miss Walker, but you needn't worry. Given your track record, I have no doubt of your success." The bell rang, and Robin picked up her books.

"Mrs. Peach making you worried, Fi?" Tony asked, packing his bag.

Peach! That was it! "Why should I be worried? I mean, yes! I'm worried," Robin admitted, exasperated. "We have this big exam—the Eleven Plus—and depending on our grade, we either go to technical school or grammar school. But I still don't understand the difference between them, and no one will tell me!"

Tony nodded. "Technical school is more like job training. Like if you want to be a mechanic or something. Grammar school is for kids who plan on going to university."

"Oh." The immensity of the Eleven Plus exam finally hit home. If Robin had to take the exam and failed, she could ruin Fiona Walker's whole life. She tried to picture Fiona in overalls, her manicured nails poking around a greasy car engine. Probably NOT what Fiona had planned. Robin shook her head. "Weird. Really weird."

"How so?" Tony asked.

"Well, the word *technical* makes technical school sound hard, but it's for kids who fail. Meanwhile *grammar school* is for smart kids, which makes no sense, either. In other places—like America for instance—*grammar school* is another word for elementary school. So it sounds really easy, but it's not."

Tony nodded. "Well, American schools have some confusing terms, too."

Robin put her hands on her hips. "Like what?"

"Well, here we're in sixth form, because it's our sixth year of school. In America, we'd have done six years of school, too, but we'd be in fifth grade. Because for some reason, they call the first year of school 'kindergarten.'"

Huh.

Outside the school, the Routemaster was already squealing to a stop. Sheila climbed onto the bus first, grabbing Robin's hand. "Fi! Let's get our favorite seats!" Robin smiled to herself as she let Sheila drag her up the narrow staircase—had she, ordinary little Robin, possibly made something *cool*? But on the upper deck, only one bench was available in the front. Two elderly tourists, a man and a lady, were already sitting on the other side, poring over a map. Sheila snagged the available bench and let go of Robin's hand. "Sorry, this seat's for Dave. You and Rupert will just have to fend for yourselves." *So much for coolness*, Robin thought as she plopped down in the row behind the elderly tourists. Rupert slid in beside her, looking annoyed. He leaned over and said in his sweetest voice, "Sorry, are you by chance lost? Might I be of service?"

The gray-haired lady looked up and smiled. "Why, aren't you charming! Ed, dear, do you hear this young man's accent? He's so cute!" She shuffled her map and a bus schedule. "We're American," she said gleefully.

Rupert raised his eyebrows. "Are you? I would not have guessed."

The lady gurgled with pleasure at the possibility she might be mistaken for a native Brit. "My grandparents were English. Maybe some of it rubbed off. Anyway, will this bus take us to Kilburn? Ed has a friend there, from the war. We're supposed to meet him for tea."

"Oh, dear," Rupert sighed. He reached up and rang the bell for the bus to stop. "You're well out of your way. I'm afraid you need to get off and walk—"

Robin interrupted. "Are you sure? Isn't Kilburn—

Ow!" Rupert kicked her! Robin stared at him in disbelief. She could see Dave and Sheila across the aisle, smothering giggles. Rupert remained focused on the elderly couple.

Rupert gave the couple a LONG list of directions as the bus lurched to a halt. The old couple hurried off. Once they were gone, Dave and Sheila guffawed out loud.

Robin turned to Rupert, horrified. "Why did you send them in the wrong direction?"

"Because they were in your seat." He flopped down into the vacated window spot and patted the seat for her to join him.

Dave called out, "And because they were American!"

"Yes, there is that." Rupert nodded.

"I thought Americans are supposed to be our friends," Robin argued.

Rupert smiled. "Well, as my dad says, 'There are friends, and then there are fat, loud, and rude friends. Americans are the latter.'"

"Agreed!" Sheila crowed.

Robin flushed—she wasn't fat, loud, and rude—was she? Okay, the old couple were a little on the heavy side, but they weren't rude. Since she was an American, too—sort of—she felt like she should defend them. Or at least get off the bus and rescue them. Out the window, she saw them, arm in arm, hobbling down the street. Rupert waved. The lady called, "Thank you."

Robin hesitated. If she spoiled the prank, Rupert, Dave, and Sheila probably wouldn't be her friends anymore. She'd have nobody at school.

Sheila smirked at her conspiratorially from across the aisle. The English girl's gesture reminded Robin of Jasmine back home. Robin thought about how mean Jasmine was to her, all the time. If she told, Sheila might target her the same way. Did she really want to endure that kind of attention as Fiona? No.

And anyway, Robin reasoned, they were Fiona's friends, not hers. She needed to do what Fiona wanted. She gave the old couple a sad little smile and waved to them halfheartedly, before turning back to her friends.

chapter eight
Liz of Ohio & Rosa of Brazil

WENDY'S ARMS WERE TIED BEHIND HER BACK. The plank loomed in front of her. But she held her head high and proud as she faced Captain Hook. "You will never catch Peter Pan!" She stomped her foot down on Hook's, to emphasize her point.

"Aghh!!!" Captain Hook groaned. Clutching his foot in his hand, he hopped around the stage.

Robin froze. "Did I hurt you? I'm so sorry—" But Hook waved her off.

"CUT!" Mr. Walker called from the audience as he came forward into the stage lights. "Fi! That was bril!" He turned to Captain Hook. All right there, Bob?"

Captain Hook nodded and set his foot down, a big grin on his face. "I like it! Well done, Miss Walker!" He turned to Mr. Walker, his voice eager. "Can we keep it?"

"Absolutely. Fi. From now on, you always stomp on Captain Hook's foot!"

"Okay," Robin agreed, breathless with excitement.

"Oh, one more." Mr. Walker continued, "You're moving around a lot when you talk—"

Oops. She was forgetting to be Fiona again! Jolene had already pointed this out in the Walker home! Robin nodded. "I'll try to be still—"

Mr. Walker interrupted her. "No, no, no! I love it! Keep doing it! Gives Wendy an energy she doesn't otherwise have!"

The weekend passed quickly, thanks to the double rehearsals called by Mr. Walker. Robin lived and breathed the Haymarket Theatre, chomping down a quick breakfast at the Walker house before zipping off to the theater, only to return in the evenings absolutely exhausted.

And she loved every minute of it.

Between scenes, she'd "run lines" backstage with fellow cast members, which involved repeating their lines in rapid succession, until Robin knew every line of the entire play by heart. She also drilled quick costume changes with Stef. But the best moments were those onstage, from the moment she felt the warmth of Peter's encouraging eyes, the glow of the spotlight, and heard her voice booming through the mic.

Now it was Monday evening, and the opening was a week and a day away.

Robin hustled backstage, where Stef frantically tried to adjust the underwire that was cutting into her side. Robin wondered why she'd been so anxious to have breasts, when they required these painful, painful contraptions known as bras.

Stef yanked again on the bra and the mic snagged. "Oh my gosh! I have to be on again in three minutes!" Robin said fretfully. She tried to turn for the wings.

Stef grabbed her back. "You bleed on that costume and you won't live to see curtain call," she said calmly. "Where's the cut?" she demanded.

Robin pointed. Stef slapped a Band-Aid on the scratch and adjusted the mic. "There. You've got a plaster. I'll fix the underwire later."

Hook hustled in. "Stef! Have you seen my hook?"

Stef looked at him, incredulous. "Bob! Again?" She shook her head, as Hook grabbed a plastic coat hanger, snapped off the ends, and fashioned the rest into a makeshift hook. He muttered to himself and raced out again.

Stef gave Robin a nudge. "Go on then. Oh. Wait." She reached behind her gigantic fix-everything kit and handed Robin the hook. "Slip that on the prop table for me, will you? Just once he's gone onstage." She winked. "No one insults MY actor."

As Robin made her way to the "legs"—the dark curtains inside the wings—she heard Mr. Walker, Peter, and the Lost Boys explode with laughter onstage at Hook's expense. She slipped the hook on the prop table with a giggle, unaware Hook could see her in the black lights.

At ten o'clock, they drifted to the edge of the stage for notes. "I'm pleased to say our running time is now down by nine minutes," Mr. Walker announced.

The cast burst into a thunderous round of applause. Robin joined in, pleased she knew the term *running time* and what it meant. That was how long it took the cast and crew to perform the entire play, and shorter is always better.

"Nigel, before we begin, may I share something?" Hook interjected.

"All right then, Bob. What is it?"

Hook cleared his throat and said calmly, "Well, you know how these old superstitions go, but—" He paused dramatically, making eye contact with Mr. Walker, then Robin, then Peter. "I do believe I might've seen the Man in Gray in the legs tonight."

Several cast members gasped. Mr. Walker beamed. "Really? There's good news. Absolutely wonderful."

Robin didn't understand. She knew what the legs were, but which actor was the Man in Gray?

Hook spotted her confusion and nodded. "Your father's never told you about the Man in Gray, Miss Fiona? Shame on him. He's a ghost." Robin gave him a doubting look, but Hook nodded again and continued. "Many years ago, the body of a nobleman in gray clothes was discovered in a false wall of the Drury Lane Theatre. He'd been stabbed to death," he added darkly. "No one knows who he was, or who did it, but they say that from time to time, he appears. And historically, his appearances predict a successful show. I believe the turnaround in your performance has a lot to do with him gracing us here tonight. You've become a truly original Wendy and I just want to say on behalf of all of us, we thank you."

Robin shuddered at the ghost story, but later that night, lying in Fiona's bed, Hook's kind words put a big smile on her face. No one had been harder on her than Hook, so his words of praise felt like a true measure of just how far she'd come. She couldn't wait for rehearsal the following night.

In truth, the play was the only time Robin got to relax and have fun. Being Fiona at school and at the Walker home was hard, because Fiona was so quiet and still. Acting that way made Robin itchy. As Wendy, she got to talk and act like herself. And they loved it! She couldn't wait for opening night! Only one more week!!!

Her thoughts drifted to the Wishers. Neera's letter had probably reached Fiona by now. At any moment, Fiona might follow Neera's instructions to find a computer, join the Wisher page, and demand to go home.

Actually, Robin realized, that might already have happened. When was the last time she had checked Facebook? Thursday. Four whole days.

Robin felt a pang of guilt. She'd been enjoying herself so much as Fiona that the few times she could've snagged the computer, she found herself opting to do other things, like grab a sandwich in the kitchen, or chat on the phone with Rupert.

She slid out of bed and listened to Mrs. Walker's snoring at the top of the stairs before tiptoeing down. She had to make contact. Had to.

As she logged on, she spotted Fiona's email icon in the corner of the screen. She hadn't tried to access it since that first day—she still didn't know the password. But Rupert had said he was going to send her an email tonight; he'd expect Fiona to have read it by tomorrow. She clicked on the icon and the mailbox demanded a password. Robin realized she had some new options to try, since she now knew Fiona's birthday. Everybody used their birthdays in passwords! Robin typed in FIONA314. Still didn't work. Wait! Robin blushed, remembering from school that British dates are written in reverse—day, then month. She typed in FIONA 143. The computer churned, and the mailbox announced she had forty-six unread messages. Wow!

Rupert had not emailed. Robin was about to shut the page again, but she was too curious to resist scrolling down Fiona's inbox. After all, what if there was something important she needed to know?

There were many emails from Sheila, mostly

about shopping. A couple more were homework questions from other kids, but at least ten of the emails were in Chinese—or Japanese—Robin wasn't really sure which. Since no one had said anything about Fiona knowing either language, Robin assumed they were sent to her by mistake and deleted them.

Finally, she flipped on to Facebook. Her eyes widened in surprise as the Wisher Network appeared before her, loaded with postings. At a quick glance, Robin spotted three new faces on the Wall, including the Samantha De Groot she'd emailed a few nights before! She'd forgotten! Liz was from Ohio, and Rosa was from Brazil. She smiled as she clicked on the chat room window—Neera was online!

WHAT'S GOING ON?

OMG—you're here! Where u bn?

Robin excused herself casually. SORRY, SORRY, SORRY!!! THEY STILL HAVE SCHOOL HERE. PLUS, I HAVE REHEARSALS FOR THE PLAY RIGHT AFTER SCHOOL. HARD 2 GET COMPUTER TIME. ARE THESE GIRLS WHAT I THINK THEY ARE?

The answer made her heart leap. Yes! Wishers! & we have u to thank for finding them!!! U did it!

Pleased but mystified, Robin typed back, WHAT DID I DO?

U emailed Dori our site—that's Samantha De Groot's real name. Dori Simpson. From Hawaii. How did u find her, BTW? Anyway, she friended us and introduced us to Liz. Then Liz brought Rosa.

Robin was typing before she finished reading.

DO ANY OF THEM KNOW FIONA?

Negative.

Negative? Since when did Neera sound so American? So much like Wrenn?

Liz and Rosa are what Alia calls a straight switch—they're in each other's bodies. Hold on a sec—don't go!!!

Robin waited and grew bored. Neera was taking forever! She read through some of the new Wishers wall posts.

Frustrated from a day in Brazil, Liz Schott from Ohio posted: *What the heck is offsides??? I don't get soccer.*

Brazilian Rosa shot back: *AS OPPOSED TO . . . CHEERLEADING? HOW IS THAT EVEN A SPORT? AND ALL THAT BOUNCING HURTS, BTW!*

Rosa, haven't u heard of a sports bra? It's in my sock drawer.

HOW WOULD I KNOW THAT? I NEVER EVEN HAD 2 WEAR A TRAINING BRA BEFORE!

When Robin's giggle turned into a yawn she checked the clock. Where was Neera anyway? What was she doing? And where was Alia? Feeling out of the loop, she checked the chat room again. Dori popped up.

Hi!

HELLO, DORI. I'M ROBIN . . . NOW FIONA WALKER. HOW R U?

OMG—ur Robin! Dying to talk to u. Thks for the FB site! Very cool! Whre u bn?

I HAD TO REHEARSE FOR A PLAY.

Really? That's so cool!!! For school?

NO, PROFESSIONAL PLAY IN LONDON.

Awesome!!!!!! Any big stars?

ONE THAT I'VE SEEN IN MOVIES. HE PLAYS PETER PAN.

Cool. Ur the only grl seems like me.

WHAT DO U MEAN?

Neera, Alia, Rosa, Liz...Want 2 go home. I lv this!!! Nvr going home.

Robin startled at the words *never going home.* She typed back.

REALLY? WHAT ABOUT SAMANTHA? THE GIRL WHOSE BODY UR IN?

Haven't heard frm her. Guess she doesn't want 2 go home, either.

Dori's answer freaked Robin out. The idea of never going home had not occurred to her. Sure, she wanted to do the play, but she did want to go home to her family in North Carolina. Eventually. Were there other Wishers like Dori? What if one of them was in Neera's body? Anxious, she typed in Neera's chat room again.

Y S T?

Y.

FIONA? HAVE U HEARD FRM HER? DID SHE GET THE SNAIL MAIL?

Don't know. Haven't heard anything!

WHAT R U DOING THAT'S KEEPING U SO LONG?

Trying 2 organize a wish—Liz and Rosa. U said we needed to learn about wishing. They r a straight switch & want 2 go home now. If they go first we can see if it works b4 you, me, and Fiona try.

The front door slammed and Robin glanced up. Jo threw her backpack onto the floor. "Unbelievable. Can't even use the computer at midnight. Out, scoot!"

Having an older sister wasn't like Robin thought it would be. Or at least, Jolene wasn't. Jolene always called her "runt," even though they were virtually the same size. And her Post-it notes were all over the house: *"Leave off my flat iron." "DON'T TOUCH!" "This Means You, runt!"* Robin didn't understand why this girl hated her so much. She'd tried being extra nice to Jo, she'd apologized for the toothbrush, and she'd done her best to stay out of Jo's way, but nothing worked.

"All right, I'll just be another minute," Robin responded in a voice that was far more polite than Jolene deserved. She went back to Neera.

MUST GO. FIND OUT.

Jolene grabbed the mouse away from Robin's hand. "Now, runt."

"Hey!" Robin tried to grab the mouse back, but Jolene pulled it out of reach. "I'll be done in a second! Just let me finish!"

"Fi! I need the computer now! Now shove OFF."

Jolene used her body like a wrecking ball, knocking Robin out of the desk chair and onto the floor.

"Hey!" Robin protested.

Jo sat down hard on the seat, adjusted the screen toward herself. Her eyebrows lifted in surprise. "What's THIS now?"

Facebook! Robin hadn't managed to close out the page! She cried, "Don't touch that!" as she tried to grab the mouse again, but Jolene was faster. She held the mouse aloft while she eagerly read the screen.

"Ooh! Somebody's in trouble! You know you're not supposed to be on Facebook, and here you are, all lit up! And with a big picture, too!"

Robin sagged. "It's not what you think."

"Isn't it? Oh, there's even a PUBLIC page! Let's see what that looks like, shall we?" Jolene clicked on the link. "Trolling for boys? I can see you've already heard from one . . . and he's eighteen, too!"

OMG! The boy who'd asked if Fiona dated! He was still on the wall!

An evil smile came onto Jo's face. "Let's ask Mum what she thinks in the morning, shall we?" She hit the PRINT button.

Robin guessed that as liberal as Mrs. Walker was, she was still a mom. She might take one look at the wall invitation from an older boy and assume the worst. If Mrs. Walker cut off her access to

Facebook, she'd have to wait on emails from Neera, or use the phone when no one was around. Neither option seemed particularly good. Admitting to herself she was busted, Robin surrendered. "Please, Jolene. I've got to have this page. I'll do anything you want."

Jolene grinned. "Anything I want? Hmmm. I want the computer. If I come in the room, you go. No argument."

Robin sighed. She was going to have to stay up even later than midnight, just to talk to Neera. But what choice did she have? "Okay."

"I'm not finished. And the bathroom. Same rules. And . . . the play." Robin looked up in amazement. Jolene's eyes were cold. "Quit," she demanded.

"No!"

Jolene picked up the Facebook printout. When Robin and Aaron got in these kind of fights, Robin could always cut off his demands by threatening to reveal one of his secrets, too. But Robin didn't have any dirt on Jolene—Fiona did. So if Robin wanted to keep her Facebook page, she was at the mercy of this merciless older sister.

"What's the problem, girls?" Mrs. Walker stood in the doorway, wrapped in a big white robe, her arms crossed. Jolene held the Facebook printout in her hand and looked expectantly at Robin.

Robin answered Mrs. Walker, but kept her eyes on Jolene. "Nothing, we're *okay.*"

Mrs. Walker sniffed. "Pipe down, then. Fi, get to bed." She gestured to Robin, intent on making sure she went to her room. Robin reluctantly followed her up the stairs. At the top, she turned to look at Jolene. Fiona's older sister was holding up a piece of paper with large letters scrawled across it:

YOU HAVE 24 HOURS.

chapter nine

Fiona Walker of London, United Kingdom, turns up

TUESDAY MORNING, ROBIN WATCHED HER baked beans fall off the back of the fork for the third time and dropped her silverware back on the plate in frustration. She felt like giving up, even though she was hungry. She'd finally found an English breakfast she liked: baked beans on toast. Now if she could only manage to *eat it*, everything would be hunky-dory.

In England, baked beans on toast are eaten with a knife and fork. Ever since Rupert, Dave, and Sheila had teased her about her table manners, she'd been trying to eat the English way, but it wasn't as easy it looked. British people didn't just hold their silverware in opposite hands. They also used their forks upside down, piling the food on the rounded side of the fork. Which made getting it in your mouth really tricky. Every time she tried, gravity took over, toppling the food back onto the plate.

Engrossed in her cutlery, Robin didn't hear the phone ring. Mrs. Walker picked it up with a rather impatient hello. She listened for half a second before rolling her eyes. "Sorry, you've got the wrong exchange. I'm sorry, I don't speak any Chinese." She hung up and turned to Robin, exasperated. "That's at least the fifth time! She doesn't speak any bloody English, so I'm sure she'll call again. Absolutely maddening." She did a double take. "What did you do to your uni? I just washed that."

Robin followed Mrs. Walker's pointing finger to her chest—the white shirt of her uniform was splattered in multiple places with baked-bean juice. She'd have to change before she left for school. She silently resolved to eat only finger foods from now on.

Racing upstairs, she ripped off the dirty shirt and scrounged for another. But something seemed to be banging on the walls of her mind. She'd missed something, she was sure of it.

When the phone rang again it worked like an alarm on her still half-asleep brain. The emails! Fiona had received a bunch of emails in Chinese! And now someone who spoke Chinese kept calling the Walker house! Robin gasped and checked the clock: she'd have to risk missing the bus, but this was important. She buttoned up her shirt and zipped downstairs to the computer, logged in to Fiona's email, and hit the RECENTLY DELETED button.

The messages were still there. Five more were in the inbox. Robin printed them all. She had no idea how to translate them, but she could already guess whom they were from and what they might say. She hit REPLY on one and simply wrote:

R U FIONA? and punched SEND.

Although Robin had found Neera via her own email address, it had never occurred to her that Fiona might be trying to get in touch with *her* the exact same way. She'd been too focused on Facebook. But now she knew Fiona Walker wasn't allowed on Facebook, so maybe it hadn't occurred to her to check there. Most likely, Fiona had emailed herself and called home, just as Robin had. But unlike Robin, Fiona's efforts were hampered by the fact she was in the body of a Chinese girl, whose words came out in a totally different language. Robin remembered the morning she'd arrived in England and how difficult she'd found it to speak with just an American accent—a different language had to be absolutely impossible.

Mrs. Walker chose that moment to wander in. "Oi! What're you still doing here! Bus! School! Right now! Your dad's not a taxi service!" Robin grabbed the printed emails, as Mrs. Walker shooed her out the door. She caught the bus just as it was pulling away and stepped aboard, breathless with excitement. She'd found Fiona! Well, okay, she didn't know for sure, but she was pretty convinced she had.

She looked again at the emails in her hand. She needed someone to translate them. School was the most likely place she'd find help. But who? Fuzzy? The headmaster? No way! Robin had no idea what the emails actually said—what if they totally gave her away? A teacher might call the Walkers. She needed a kid, but not Rupert, Sheila, or Dave. *They'd* text each other in minutes and say she was crazy. And was it too terrible to admit, Robin wondered, that she wanted to be Rupert's girlfriend for just the teensiest bit longer?

Robin was still wracking her brain as the school coasted into view. She spotted a familiar face on the steps and practically threw herself off the still-moving bus, trying to catch up to the short, but incredibly sweet boy who'd helped her ever since she'd arrived at Clarendon School—Tony Newsome.

"This is Japanese, not Chinese," Tony declared, handing the email back to Robin.

"SHHH!!!!" Robin looked up at the annoyed librarian. Some things were the same all over the world.

They were supposed to be researching the native home of the snow leopard for geography. As Tony pulled another book from the shelf and pretended to read, Robin whispered, "How do you know?"

"We lived in Tokyo when I was little, remember?" Tony answered.

"So you speak Japanese?" she asked him eagerly.

He looked at her like she was bonkers. "I was three! Use Babel Fish."

"Babble what?"

"Babel Fish," he said again, as though it were the most obvious thing in the world. "Online translation site."

"How do you spell it? Can you write it down?"

As Tony reached for his pen, Robin heard another student rounding the stacks. Fearing it might be Rupert or his friends, she shifted away from Tony and grabbed a book, pretending to be deeply engrossed.

Robin thought she'd been subtle, but Tony sighed. "We used to be friends, Fi. You sat one desk away from me from second form all the way through last year. We went to each other's birthday parties and ate cakes in front of the telly every Friday afternoon. All of a sudden, you're tall and popular, I'm short and"—he fumbled for a word that wouldn't wound his pride— "not. Now you can't even be seen talking to me because your new friends might see you?" He threw down the pen. "Look it up for yourself."

As he walked away, Robin called after him quietly. "Tony." He stopped and slowly turned around. "It's not what you think."

He looked right into her eyes. "Isn't it? Been the same all year." He pushed on the door without another glance.

Messages in a bottle. That's how Fiona's first two emails read to Robin, as she sat at the Walker computer that afternoon and translated them on Babel Fish. Fiona reminded her of Robinson Crusoe—the sailor stranded on a deserted island, who stuffed notes into bottles and threw them into the surf, in the unlikely hope someone would read them and rescue him. On Monday, Fiona had written:

> Whoever is reading this, please call me. I'm Fiona Walker of Queen's Park, London, even if I don't look like her. My exchange is 78978262 in Japan. Ask for Naomi Nagata.

Tuesday:

> I know that I still exist. If I didn't exist, my email would've been returned, because there wouldn't be any fwalker143. It hasn't, so someone is reading this. Whoever you are, please write back. Or call. Again, Naomi Nagata, exchange 78978262. I don't know the code to dial Japan, but I'm sure you can get my mum to help you. Don't worry, my mum's really nice.

Robin was just picking up the phone to try and dial Fiona when Babel Fish pinged through again— Thursday's email.

> Are you Naomi? Did you do this to me on purpose? Is that why you won't answer me?

Or did this happen by accident, but now you really like being me? Can't say as I blame you, Naomi, because your life STINKS. You've got 24 hours to make contact with me, or I'll start bloody calling. I'll tell my mum that you're not me and I'll prove it. And when I do, my mum will turn on you so fast that . . .

Robin put the handset down again. Maybe she wasn't in such a hurry to reach Fiona after all. She glanced through the rest of the emails. Yesterday, Fiona had started sending one email every hour. The last five all had the same word on them. She clicked on the translation.

THIEF.
THIEF.
THIEF.
THIEF.
THIEF.

Heat rushed to Robin's face. She was embarrassed and angry. Who did this girl think she was? She couldn't believe she'd gone to this much trouble, just to find the incredibly rude, incredibly ungrateful Fiona Walker. The more Robin thought, the angrier she got. She'd worked hard to maintain Fiona's life this week. She'd gone to Fiona's school, maintained Fiona's relationship with her boyfriend, and even learned an entire play! All so Fiona's life would look the same when she got home. And all this girl could do was call her a THIEF?

A Facebook chat window popped up—Neera.

Good! Ur there! Where did u go last night?

LONG STORY.

K. Did Fiona contact u?

Robin started typing, YES! I FOUND HER . . . but abruptly deleted it. She stared at the question on the screen for a long time. Finally, she wrote back:

NO. DID SHE CONTACT U?

No. The disappointment in Neera's single-syllable response was clear. **Robin, I don't know what to do—**

Uncomfortable with having lied, Robin felt absolutely desperate to get off the computer. She interrupted Neera's thought.

WHAT HAPPENED 2 ROSA AND LIZ BTW? DID THEY SWITCH?

They were going 2, and then

Robin didn't let Neera finish.

HAVE 2 GO 2 REHEARSAL. MY RIDE IS WAITING OUTSIDE.

Another lie! She didn't have to go to rehearsal for another fifteen minutes.

Robin, wait! U keep disappearing and I'm not going to be able to—

I'LL BE ONLINE AFTER REHEARSAL. PROMISE.

She switched the computer off, just so she wouldn't have to lie again.

Robin wandered into the kitchen and grabbed a

Ribena. The raspberry-flavored British drink wasn't a soda or juice but something in between. It was absolutely delicious.

Robin tried to think about the situation logically. Why had she lied? She'd found Fiona. She was Naomi Nagata of Japan. That meant there were at least four Wishers in their network, not three like they'd originally thought. The real Naomi Nagata was probably in Neera's body.

Robin knew from Fiona's emails that she was afraid, and sometimes fear made people mean. Robin's dad had taught her that the day she'd found a baby squirrel, dragging one of its rear legs. Robin had yelled to him for help, as she tried to corner the tiny creature. Just as she reached down to scoop it up, her dad swatted her hand away, hard—a second before the squirrel snapped his sharp little teeth right where her fingers had been. Her dad had looked at her and said, "A scared animal is a mean one, sweetie."

That's what was bugging her! Right now, Fiona was like the squirrel. If she told Fiona about the Wisher Network, Fiona would probably demand to go home immediately—as in *today*. And Neera, being Neera, would be way too nice to refuse. They'd both insist on wishing that moment, even if wishing meant Neera ended up in Naomi Nagata's body, instead of going home. Even if it meant Robin never got to do *Peter Pan*.

The Ribena abruptly clogged in her throat.

Was that why she'd lied? Because she just wanted to

do the play? Robin did a mental checklist of her emotions. Yes, she really did want to do the play! Desperately! She'd worked so hard and she was good—everyone said so! They also said how horrible Fiona was! Okay, they didn't say it like *that*, but that's what they meant.

Once. She just wanted to perform in the play one time. And opening night was only one week away.

A thought oozed its way into Robin's brain: what if she kept Neera and Fiona apart for a few more days? She'd already lied to Neera. She could email Fiona back. Stall. Tell her she had no idea how this happened or why. Robin could do the play opening night, and look for Naomi Nagata in the meantime. Jo's ultimatum tickled Robin's conscience—another reason why this plan might not work—but Robin couldn't solve *every* problem on the spot. She'd deal with Jo later. Anyway, if the Wishers were *all* going to get home like they originally planned, they still had to get in touch with Naomi. In fact, Robin decided, she wasn't lying to Neera so much as she was *protecting* her.

Outside, Mr. Walker beeped his horn. Rehearsal time! She stuffed the Ribena back in the fridge. En route to the car, Robin promised herself that she'd start looking for Naomi as soon as possible, tonight, after rehearsal. Or maybe tomorrow, since they were working late tonight. If she hadn't found Naomi by opening night, she'd come clean with everybody and beg forgiveness.

chapter ten

Neera Gupta goes on vacation

PETER PAN OPENED HIS MOUTH WIDE AND said, "Unique New York."

"Unique New York," Robin echoed, excited to realize opening night was exactly one week away. Next Tuesday, she'd be performing as Wendy in front of hundreds of people.

Peter scrunched his mouth, like he was very angry, and said, "Unique New York!" The cast followed suit, turning their eyes angrily on one another. Peter shook his fist and said it louder, "UNIQUE NEW YORK!" Robin shook her fist, too, and stomped her feet as she yelled the words. Peter nodded at her with approval. He leaned toward her and gently whispered, "Unique New York," as if those words could somehow calm her down. Robin softened, too, saying "Unique New York" like a gentle "thank you." The actors shared hugs as they made up with good tidings of "Unique New York."

Warm-ups. Robin loved them. Just like stretching before a soccer game, actors did warm-up games and tongue twisters to get their bodies and voices loose and comfortable. They pretended to be animals, squeezed hands in a circle, and said silly things. In the beginning, they were embarrassing—like when Captain Hook imitated a kitty cat. But now Robin loved the games as much as she loved every moment onstage and mostly because the adults played along. Back home, any time Robin had tried to get her parents to play a pretend game, they'd always made excuses like needing to cook dinner or help with homework. But these adults threw themselves into every game. They didn't care if they looked silly, and their knack for details and ability to change the game without pause made every moment perfect fun.

"Grand!" Peter announced. "Now, move about the stage—in any direction—with the words 'red leather, yellow leather.' If you encounter anyone, you must pivot in another direction."

Robin found her repetitions of "red leather, yellow leather" turning into "rellow ledder" at the same moment as she crashed into the boy who played John, Wendy's brother. They both spun around, spewing "red thether" as they fell on top of each other.

Peter admonished them as he drifted past. "Red leather!"

"Yellow lea— AH!!!" Robin and John fell over again, this time deliberately. Sometimes it was fun just to fall. But John's sword, which he'd been brandishing throughout the warm-ups, flew sideways, hitting Peter in the knees. Peter tilted, his arms rotating like windmills as he fell. He yelled, "Red leather!" as though it was "Remember the Alamo!" and plunged to the floor. Robin and John scrambled to safety, laughing so hard tears formed in Robin's eyes. Lying on the floor, Peter rasped, "Red leath . . ." as Captain Hook grabbed John's sword and thrust it between Peter's arm and chest. Peter feigned a death rattle.

"YELLOW LEATHER!" Captain Hook hooted in victory, holding the sword above his head like a trophy. He turned the weapon on Robin and John. "Makeup," Hook declared, "anyone late gets me dagger." They screamed and fled, elbowing each other in their haste to be the first into the dressing rooms.

Backstage, pink-mohawked Stef stuffed Robin into Wendy's costume and led her to makeup. She stared into Robin's eyes, eyeliner pencil at the ready. "Oi! Fiona! Eyes on the floor," she ordered. "You've been in a trance since rollers. Penny for your thoughts."

"I'm thinking," Robin admitted. She'd been contemplating how she could get in touch with Naomi when she got back to the Walker household later that night. "Can you mail a laptop to India?" Robin asked.

Stef's eyebrows rose. "I suppose so," she answered. "But why would you want to?"

"I uh . . . have this last school project," Robin said.

Boy, she was getting good at lying. "A social studies—" Robin saw Stef's eyebrows rise again and stopped herself. Wrong term! She wracked her brain—what was social studies called in England? "Um, I mean, humanities project."

Stef sighed. "All right, then. What do you need to do? Eyes left."

Robin shifted her eyes and continued, "Say you had to get in touch with someone in a fishing village in India. You don't know this person, and she doesn't have a phone or a computer, and she doesn't speak English. What would you do?"

"Ah, Six Degrees of Separation!" Stef looked impressed. "You have one very hip teacher—"

"Sorry," Robin interrupted. "Six what?"

"Six Degrees of Separation. It's a theory that we're only six people apart from anyone else in the world. Like, I may not know Barack Obama personally, but let's say I had to get in touch with him. I go through a list of everyone I know, and who they know. Hmm... I once did Alex Kingston's makeup. So I know her, and she was once married to Ralph Fiennes. Ralph Fiennes worked for Steven Spielberg on his movie *Schindler's List*. Steven Spielberg knows Barack Obama. I call Alex, then Ralph, then Steven, and voilà, Obama. That's four degrees of separation. Trick is figuring out what six people are between you and the girl in the fishing village." She pulled out a lip liner and lifted Robin's face. "Lips now, no talking, darling." Robin closed her mouth and Stef drew with the pencil. "S'on Facebook, you know."

At the mere mention of Facebook, Robin sputtered, "What!" and moved, causing Stef to draw a line of pink straight across her cheek.

Stef groaned. "Jolly great. Now I've got to get that off and do your cheek again. Hold still! Not going to talk if you're going to flop around." She rubbed off the lipstick.

"Sorry," Robin choked. "Umm . . . what about Facebook?"

Stef started reapplying. "Six Degrees, the Facebook Experiment. It's on the home page. They're trying to get every member of Facebook worldwide to log into it and say hello to the world. You can see postings from everywhere. All you have to do is join the experiment, then find someone who lives near the fishing village, send them a message, and ask them to pass it to the girl. Throw that one at your teacher. Bet she'll be impressed. There. Humanities are officially over. Now can we return to *Peter Pan?*" Stef cast her a withering look.

By way of an answer, Robin reached out and hugged her.

A muffled Stef said, "Blimey, you must be flunking."

Robin could hear Peter sending Tinkerbell away for how she'd treated Wendy. Meanwhile, backstage, she hustled around trying to find John. They had to be onstage in two minutes, and recently, he'd been late for every entrance. She finally found him in the hallway between the greenroom and the wings and whispered, "Why are you waiting here? C'mon!" She gestured toward the legs, the two-story-high black curtains that shrouded the actors in the wings.

"I'm scared," the younger boy admitted.

"Of what?" Robin asked.

"The ghost. That Man in Gray bloke. What if he's around? I don't want to wait in those big black curtains. I'm staying here."

Robin nodded. The truth was the story of the Man in Gray scared her, too, especially since even the grown-ups seemed to believe this ghost was real. But she had no intention of admitting that to John. She offered him a hand. "There's no such thing as ghosts, but we can wait in the legs together if you like."

John nodded shyly and took her hand. Seeing them, the stage manager mouthed a "phew" and moved swiftly on. Tucked inside the darkened curtains, Robin found a spot between the pulley ropes where they would still have a little light from the stage.

Suddenly, a deep voice moaned, "UGHHH . . ."

The gigantic black curtains suddenly grew arms—arms that were slowly reaching out for Robin. The Man in Gray!

"AUGH!" John and Robin screamed in unison. All

activity onstage stopped, the actors turning to see the commotion in the wings. The stage manager and the prop master raced over to find out what was going on.

The ghost started laughing hysterically, his hands reaching to lift the curtain away. Captain Hook! The actor was absolutely choking with laughter. "Revenge! That'll teach you to steal my hook!" he guffawed, just as he tripped on the pulley cables, knocking some of the weights off. One of the cables ripped skyward. Hook grabbed for it, but missed. Everyone's eyes craned upward in alarm.

The large set pieces for the play—like the wardrobe, the bed, and the ship—were suspended in the rafters by cables and weights when they weren't in use onstage. The cable Hook had dislocated was attached to the headboard of the brass bed of the opening scene. Once the cable whipped free, the bed tilted precariously. The bedcovers slid off and floated down to the stage.

"CLEAR THE STAGE!" Mr. Walker barked, just as the bed started falling in fits and starts, pulled by gravity like a huge mountain climber rappelling down a cliff face while the actors hustled out of the way.

Finally, the brass headboard reached the stage with a terrible *CRUNCH*.

It took only ten minutes for the running crew to break down the bed, but an hour for Mr. Walker to sort out who was responsible. Moments after Captain Hook finger-pointed Robin for stealing his hook, Stef admitted she was the culprit, which only escalated the argument. Robin was surprised to hear how much these grown-ups sounded like her and Jo when they were fighting. Mr. Walker rolled his eyes at the bickering and finally shushed them. He informed Stef and Captain Hook that they would be spending the night at the theater with him, either repairing the bed or searching for a new one. Alternatively, they could look for new jobs in the morning.

As he dropped Robin off at the Walker home, he'd kissed her forehead and said, "Good night, my darling," as he unlocked the front door for her. "Get some rest, you did well. Not to worry about the bed, not your fault. I'll find another." He pushed open the door, telling her, "Lock it behind you," and headed back to the car.

Jo was sitting at the computer desk as Robin walked in. Her eyes narrowed on Robin, but quickly swept past her. "Where's Dad?" she asked.

"Going back to work. Part of the set collapsed," Robin started. "You should have seen it—"

Robin paused, surprised at the disappointment that lined the older girl's face. Was she upset because her dad hadn't come inside? Robin started to feel sorry for her, until Jo spat, "Guess Mum and Dad will just have to read this tomorrow morning then," as she flapped the Facebook page at Robin. "Your time is UP."

Robin met her eyes, trying to appear more confident than she felt. "Show it to them. Because I'm not quitting." To prove her mettle, Robin moved to the computer. "Are you done here?"

Jo placed her hands on her hips and stared at Robin, openmouthed. "Should've known you were stalling." She stood up and blocked the way to the computer. "I suppose you intend to tell them I tried to steal the part, right?"

Robin's eyes grew wide. Jo was the understudy for Wendy! So that was why she was always angry—she wanted the part! But why had Mr. Walker picked Fiona over Jo? Robin had no idea.

Jo took her silence as a confession and sank into the desk chair. "No, I'm not bloody done here."

As little as Robin liked Jolene Walker, she felt the tiniest smidge of sympathy for her. She knew how Jo felt, exactly the way Robin had felt when her mom suggested Sophie could swim in her place at the conference meet. She tried a softer tone. "Look, Jo—"

"Just go away, runt!" Robin could hear the crack in Jo's voice, but she nodded and went upstairs to Fiona's room, where she tried to stay awake. She was exhausted, but she needed to get online. She'd promised Neera she wouldn't disappear, but now she couldn't get on the computer.

At midnight, the chill of sleep shuddered through

her body and refused to let go. Her head grew heavy, her focus dim. At last she fell asleep in the beanbag chair.

The stinging sound of an alarm clock shook Robin awake early Wednesday morning—Mrs. Walker had obviously grown tired of her being late to school.

Wait! It was morning! She'd missed Neera again! Robin raced all the way downstairs before she remembered that North Carolina was five hours behind England. It was the middle of the night in Concord—Neera would be sound asleep.

Feeling guilty, Robin decided to look for Naomi in India. Just as Stef had promised, the Six Degrees Facebook Experiment was on the Facebook home page. It was so easy she thought the whole project would be a piece of cake. But scrolling through all those names, Robin realized she'd had no idea what two million people looked like!

Robin heard footsteps upstairs—the Walkers were awake. She'd have to get ready for school. Suddenly, Samantha De Groot's beautiful face appeared onscreen.

Hello, Robin! How's the show?

HEY, DORI. WHY R U ON THE COMPUTER SO EARLY?

Bored.

HAVE U TALKED TO NEERA OR ALIA TODAY?

No. R u doing interviews yet?

Robin smiled, happy that someone shared her excitement about the play. She typed, YES! TOMORROW! SOME MAGAZINE CALLED TIME OUT!

Cool beans! Mention your good friend Samantha in South Africa.

K. HEY, DORI, I GOTTA GO. GOTTA TRY AND FIND NEERA AND ALIA.

Bye.

Robin was about to race upstairs and get dressed, but she couldn't resist checking the Wisher page. The "straight switch" Wishers had been fighting.

Rosa: U SAID I could have it!

Liz: Did not! U just mailed my iPod to yourself! I'm mailing it BACK!!!

Robin scrolled through the argument, which went on for pages. Rosa and Liz sure had a lot to say about an iPod. She could see postings from Alia and Neera, too. They'd tried to moderate the fight, but Liz and Rosa were so mad they refused to wish themselves home. Over an iPod. Robin's disappointment turned to panic as she read Neera's next response.

Rosa, Liz, please. Let's solve this. Alia and I won't be around 2 help for a week! My—er, Robin's—family is going to the beach & they've invited Alia 2. I don't know if there's a computer there. Robin, if ur reading this, I've got the chat room on, in hope u will answer. Can't believe u ditched me again.

The annual beach trip. Robin had forgotten her family vacation. She checked the clock—yes, they were gone. Why hadn't Neera said anything before? Robin thought back to how she'd cut Neera off before rehearsal. It was her own fault. But would they really just leave her for a week? Tears welled in her eyes.

She'd brought this on herself. She'd found Fiona and lied about it, keeping the information to herself, just so she could drag out her time here in England and do the play. Her thoughts had been as selfish as the two Wishers fighting over an iPod. She'd also thought that she could find Naomi herself. She'd imagined proudly introducing Neera and Fiona to each other online. Stupid, stupid, stupid.

The Sea Charm in Emerald Isle, North Carolina, did not have a computer. Robin knew that from the last three vacations she'd spent there with her family. There were only two little rooms in their suite—a main room with a kitchenette and a foldout couch for the girls to share, with Aaron on the floor in a sleeping bag. Her parents used the tiny, featureless bedroom.

Memories of that crummy inn made her jealous of Neera. Robin loved that trip. She loved the wonderfully fishy smell of the ocean that stuck to every piece of clothing. She loved building whole villages of sand castles with Sophie, until they were grimy and exhausted. She loved lingering with her mom on the beach in the evening, lazily passing control of a kite and watching the fishermen cast their lines off the pier. Her mom had called it "quality time." Robin had always thought it was a dumb phrase, but now she understood what it meant.

Her sudden longing for home was so strong she could barely breathe. Hot, salty tears poured down her face as she angrily punched the keyboard. She wasn't really sure why she cared about Rosa and Liz's fight, but it mattered a lot, actually.

ROSA AND LIZ, THIS IS ROBIN. NEERA'S IN MY BODY RIGHT NOW, AND I'M FIONA WALKER IN LONDON. ROSA, I'LL GIVE U MY IPOD. U CAN HAVE IT. JUST POST UR ADDRESS IN BRAZIL AND I'LL SEND IT. THERE. FIGHT OVER. YOU'RE MAKING A BIG MISTAKE BY FIGHTING WITH EACH OTHER RATHER THAN TRYING 2 GO HOME. I KNOW BECAUSE I MADE A BIG MISTAKE 2. HUGE. LIKE U, I STARTED LIKING ALL THE THINGS FIONA HAS. LIKE A REALLY CUTE BOYFRIEND AND A STARRING ROLE IN A PLAY—A PROFESSIONAL ONE! FIONA'S SMART AND PRETTY, AND I'M NOT. YESTERDAY, I LIED TO SOMEONE, JUST BECAUSE I WANTED TO STAY FIONA A LITTLE BIT LONGER. AND NOW NEERA'S GONE! SHE'S AT THE BEACH

WITH MY MOM, DAD, BROTHER, AND LITTLE
SISTER. FOR A WEEK!!! I LOVE THAT TRIP
AND I'VE MISSED IT. BUT I LOVE MY FAMILY
EVEN MORE. WHEN I REALIZED I WOULDN'T
SEE THEM FOR ANOTHER WEEK, I CRIED.
THERE'S NOTHING FIONA HAS THAT'S MORE
IMPORTANT 2 ME THAN MY FAMILY. IF THAT
MEANS ANYTHING 2 U, GO HOME WHILE YOU
CAN. WISH. SET A TIME, SO U WISH AT THE
EXACT SAME MOMENT. IF IT WORKS, LET ME
KNOW.

Robin posted her note and nearly slammed the
computer shut. She was tired and upset, but realized
she still had one thing she needed to do, if she was
going to make things right. She had to tell Fiona what
was going on.

She opened Fiona's email—a lone message in
Japanese was there, waiting to be opened. Robin clicked
on it and opened the Babel Fish site to translate. The
email began with the words:

Yes, I'm Fiona! I'm so sorry if you got
those other emails I sent. I hope you're still
talking to me! Are you in my body? Are you
Naomi? Is my family okay? Who are you? Do
you know how we might be able to get home?
Please forgive me. I'll do whatever you want
if you'll help me be Fiona again.

Robin hit REPLY and started writing, telling Fiona all she knew, starting with her own name. She reassured Fiona her family was fine, and told her about the Wisher Network on Facebook, and her plan to get them all home. She gulped as she wrote the next part:

I MESSED UP, FIONA. I DIDN'T TELL ANYBODY ABOUT FINDING YOU YESTERDAY, BECAUSE I WANTED TO DO YOUR PLAY. AND I LIKED YOUR BOYFRIEND, TOO. I LIKED BEING YOU. IN FACT, I HAD AN EASIER TIME BEING YOU THAN BEING ME. BUT THAT DOESN'T GIVE ME THE RIGHT TO DO WHAT I DID. I'M SORRY. AND NOW I CAN'T WISH MYSELF HOME UNTIL NEERA GETS BACK IN A WEEK—ON TUESDAY. BUT IF YOU WANT TO GET HOME BEFORE THEN, WE CAN TRY WISHING TOMORROW AND I'LL BE NAOMI. I'LL DO IT BECAUSE I WAS SELFISH, AND I HURT YOU.

Robin sucked in a breath as she hit SEND. She checked the time zone clock on her computer—Japan was nine hours ahead of London. It was seven in the morning in London, so it was four o'clock in the afternoon in Japan. Fiona could easily be online, so an answer might come back within minutes. She was scared to read it.

chapter eleven

Eleven Plus

"FIONA WALKER, I BOUGHT YOU THAT CLOCK for a reason!" Mrs. Walker shouted from the top of the stairs. "You'd best be ready for school!" Robin could hear her descending the steps as she continued, "You, little one, have the Eleven Plus!"

Robin's mouth dropped open. The Eleven Plus! She'd forgotten!

Robin reluctantly headed upstairs while trying to calculate the enormity of her mistake. She'd forgotten about the exam. Fiona's whole future at school depended on how she did on the Eleven Plus. If Fiona wanted to switch back, they needed to try right now, so she could save her school career.

Robin was in such a hurry to get back to the computer that she fumbled the buttons on her uniform. Yesterday's skirt was pretty rumpled, but she didn't want to waste precious time looking for a clean one. A quick brush of her hair and she called out, "I . . . um . . . have to use the bathroom!" only to remember that *bathroom* wasn't the right word. "I mean, loo!" She dashed down the stairs to the computer.

Mrs. Walker's voice followed her. "Fine! Loo, then car!"

The message was there—in Japanese! Forgot! Crikey! Babel Fish! She punched the keyboard, urging the Internet to work faster. Robin remembered it was nine hours ahead in Japan. Would Fiona even be awake? Why hadn't she thought of the exam earlier!!!! Babel Fish churned out the message in English:

I'm still in the play???? R u crazy?!! No way. & FYI, I don't even like Rupert!

A dazed Robin stared at the message. Jo had been right all along—Fiona had wanted to quit the play.

An impatient Mrs. Walker barked, "Fiona Walker!"

Robin turned and reluctantly headed for the car.

On the way to school, Mrs. Walker noticed her apprehension and softened her tone. "Now, darling, I know you're nervous. But you'll be fine on the exam. Just do your best and I'm sure you'll get top marks."

Top marks? As in the best grade? She didn't even know what was ON the exam!

Mr. and Mrs. Walker were really, really ambitious people, Robin decided. They were nice and all, and they didn't come across as ambitious, but they were. They probably had to be, in order to work in professional theater and television. From the conversations Robin had overheard backstage at the Haymarket, it was pretty tough being an actor, even if you were good.

But the Walkers had equally ambitious goals for Fiona, too. Robin had come to realize that kids usually didn't get handed starring roles. They had to try out and get rejected many times before they even got a little part. But the Walkers put Fiona in a starring role, when Robin knew from Mr. Walker's many comments that she did not have any acting experience at all. They did it because they loved her, Robin guessed, but they still expected her to succeed, too. And at the same time, Fiona was supposed to take a major exam and do well. That was expecting an awful lot.

But why didn't Fiona tell them this? Why hadn't she just told her parents she didn't want the play? Why did she keep a boyfriend she didn't even like? Why did she wish?

At first, Robin had assumed Fiona's wish was even more of an accident than her own. Robin had thought Fiona was all the things she wasn't: beautiful, smart, popular, and talented. Then it turned out Fiona wasn't talented, at least not at acting, and she knew it, too. But did she think that meant she wasn't pretty, either? Or smart? Or popular? Did she assume that because she wasn't good at one thing, she wasn't good at anything? Could Fiona possibly think something so silly? Robin didn't get it.

"Here we are! Kisses, darling." Mrs. Walker planted a big smooch on her head. "Bell must've gone off, so off you go, then. Godspeed."

Robin walked slowly up the steps, toward poor Fiona's doom. She was pretty sure she was going to flunk the Eleven Plus, because she wasn't the student who had been sitting in Fuzzy's classroom all year. Fiona was. But Fiona had refused the chance to solve her own problems, so she'd just have to live with Robin's results.

Robin pushed open the heavy fire doors of the dining hall. Summer sunshine poured through the massive windows, tilted open for air, while stagnant heat bore down onto rows of desks, moved there for the Eleven Plus.

Rupert, Dave, and Sheila fanned themselves in the second row, while Fuzzy pointed to a desk next to Tony. "You're late, Miss Walker, please take a seat."

Robin sat while Fuzzy passed out the exams. "Please keep the paper facedown until I instruct you to turn it over. You will have one hour and thirty minutes to complete this test. There will be no breaks. Anyone needing to use the facilities must speak now. Anyone?" No one spoke. "Fine. You must now contain yourself until the exam is over. Anyone asking to be excused, for any reason, will be disqualified. Any talking and you will be disqualified. Any eyes drifting near your neighbor's paper, and you will be disqualified. Once I instruct you to turn these papers over, you will focus solely on the test in front of you. Any questions?"

Rupert raised his hand. "Yes, sorry, Miss? If the fire alarm goes?"

Sheila snickered.

Fuzzy looked at him sternly. "You will be disqualified. All of you."

"Earthquake?" he shot back. Now the entire class was laughing.

"Mr. Sellars, if you persist, I will disqualify you now."

He pouted. "Yes, Miss."

"Good then. Turn them over. Clock starts now." Mrs. Peach waddled back to the front of the room and picked up her book. Robin turned the exam over with a sigh and glanced down:

1. **One** letter from the first word must be moved
   to the second word to make two new words.
   The letters must not be rearranged. **Both** new
   words must make sense.
   e.g., CLIMB LOSE **C** LIMB CLOSE

CORAL COOK

A. C
B. O
C. R
D. A
E. L

Robin couldn't believe her luck. She scanned the test. These were brain teasers! The Eleven Plus was full of brain teasers! She was GREAT at brain teasers—they were her parents' dorky idea of fun. She sighed in relief. She wasn't going to ruin the rest of Fiona's life after all. She might not get "top marks," but she was pretty confident she wouldn't flunk, either. She dug in.

Forty minutes later, Robin was cruising easily through the exam when she heard a buzzing around her ear. Without looking, she waved a hand in the air to brush off the tiny, unseen source. The buzzing stopped and then started again, as she felt a tickle on her hand. Annoyed, she glanced up.

A yellow jacket was sitting on her hand.

Robin sucked in a breath. She'd meant it when she'd told Neera she was allergic. She'd only been four when she got stung by a yellow jacket, but she still remembered the swelling and shortness of breath that followed, and her mom's panic as they rode in the ambulance.

She shut her eyes and tried to regain her composure by focusing on the positives. Maybe, as Fiona, she wasn't allergic. Robin wasn't absolutely certain this was true and she was too scared to find out.

She blew at her hand, trying to get the insect off without angering it. Beads of sweat trickled down her face. Maybe only a minute had passed—she didn't know for sure—but every moment felt like an hour. She glanced at the clock—she was losing time. She whipped her hand away and the yellow jacket launched itself and whirled angrily around her head. She picked up her exam and swatted at it.

The yellow jacket landed again, this time on her shoulder.

Out of the corner of her eye, she could see Rupert watching her. She tried to make eye contact. She was sure that as Fiona's boyfriend, he would try to help. But when Fuzzy shifted in her chair, he abruptly planted his eyes back onto his work.

The tail curled—it was going to sting her—and Robin whimpered as an impossibly swift hand flew past her face and shoulder. She glanced up.

Tony stood over her, a look of triumph on his face. He put a finger to his lips to say "shhh" and lifted his closed fist, indicating the bee was inside. He squeezed once and uncurled his hand. He dusted his hands together, knocking the yellow jacket to the floor, and stepped on it. Had he been stung?

Concerned, Robin gestured to his hand. Tony shook his head, took his seat, and focused on his test, Fuzzy none the wiser. Robin could've kissed him.

Five minutes later, she heard Tony suck in a sharp breath. She decided to risk a glance. His hand had swollen to the size of a baseball glove. Robin's eyes bored into him. Keeping his eyes on his test, he shook his head furiously. He wanted to finish the exam, but as the minutes ticked by, Robin could hear his gasps. Apparently, she wasn't the only one allergic to yellow jackets.

She wrestled with what to do. If she spoke up, she was afraid they'd both be disqualified. Fiona's and Tony's futures might both be wrecked. But she also knew from personal experience how little time Tony had.

She stared at Fuzzy, in the vain hope the teacher would sense someone was watching her. Tony's breaths were coming faster now. Robin raised her hand, but Fuzzy checked her watch and turned a page in her book. Robin swallowed bravely and finally called out, "MISS!"

The irritation in the teacher's eyes was obvious. "Miss Walker, I suppose you know what this means," she began sternly.

Robin pointed frantically at Tony. "He got stung by a yellow jacket! He's allergic!"

The teacher hustled over to him. "Mr. Newsome, I think you need to head to the nurse's office. You may re-sit the test when you've recovered." She glanced around the room. "There's no one else here to monitor. I can't leave. Can you make it to the nurse's office on your own?"

The gasping boy nodded.

Robin protested. "But Miss! He can't—"

"Miss Walker! Please. I appreciate you had to alert me to this, but your concern is now seriously endangering your status on the Eleven Plus!"

"But Miss . . ."

"NOT another word," came the clipped answer.

All the kids were staring as Robin stood up and insisted, "I'll take him."

The teacher's eyes flared. "Consider yourself disqualified, Miss Walker."

"But—" Robin started and then stopped herself. Unfair! But looking into Fuzzy's eyes, Robin realized there was no point arguing with this stupid, stupid teacher. She placed an arm around Tony, suppressing tears. She said softly, "Come on, let's get you to the nurse." Robin glared at the teacher as they started for the doors. "The headmaster will understand."

Fuzzy's back arched. As Robin pulled the heavy fire door open for Tony, the teacher called out, "Mr. Newsome, actually, I'm afraid I have to disqualify you as well."

Robin wheeled around and stared, openmouthed, but Fuzzy merely folded her arms. Robin stepped through the door and let it go—*WHAM*. For a split second, she took satisfaction in the rattling echo it made down the hall. But her satisfaction evaporated as she realized she had no idea where the nurse's office was.

Any other time, she would've gone back. She'd have swallowed her pride, opened the door, and just asked.

But she'd only had a few hours sleep and she was angrier than she'd ever been in her entire life. She was angry with Fiona for not taking this dumb test herself. She was angry at Fuzzy for refusing to help, simply because somebody might cheat while she was gone. Most of all, Robin was angry with herself, for losing her temper and putting herself in this terrible, horrible, and basically impossible situation.

But where was the nurse's office?

She spotted the fire alarm on the wall. If English schools were like American ones, firemen and ambulance workers would come right away. She yanked it, and the shrill peal felt as satisfying as a good scream. "There," she said to Tony, "now we're all disqualified." She guided him to the front steps to wait for the EMT.

chapter twelve
Liz and Rosa go home

MR. WALKER STORMED AROUND THE KITCHEN. "HOW COULD THEY EXPEL HER FOR THAT? SHE ONLY HAD TWO DAYS LEFT AT THAT SCHOOL!"

Upstairs in Fiona's room, Robin tried—hopelessly— to block out the dull roar of both Walker parents. They were pretty mad at Fuzzy. And the headmaster. And pretty much everyone they could think of.

The ambulance had come immediately, and Tony Newsome was taken to the hospital. Although the ambulance workers said she'd done the right thing, the headmaster had a different opinion. In his view, Fiona had pulled the fire alarm when there was no fire. He'd promptly called the Walkers and expelled her. Rules were rules, he said. Any student pulling the fire alarm—except in the event of fire—faced immediate expulsion. No exceptions.

Mr. Walker kissed her head fiercely in the car and told her she'd done the right thing, and Mrs. Walker hugged her at the door. Jolene merely scowled and headed to the computer while the elder Walkers took over the kitchen. They were now contemplating how they would combat Fiona's expulsion. Robin was touched by their support, but she didn't have any idea what could be done—she was guilty.

Hiding in Fiona's room, she deliberated how to break the news to Fiona. What would she say? Would she even want to come back? Robin had made an utter mess of her life. She'd kept the boyfriend Fiona didn't like, she'd committed Fiona to a role in a play, and now she'd gotten her kicked out of school and disqualified from the Eleven Plus. Did every Wisher mess up this badly? Robin doubted it. She seemed to have a special knack for dumb mistakes.

Fiona's cell interrupted her thoughts. Robin glanced at the text message.

CMING OVR

Rupert. Robin frowned. Yesterday, she would've been excited he was coming over. Now she wanted to run.

The door to her room was shoved open. Jolene stood in the hallway, her arms folded. "Do you fancy getting out of here for a while?"

Robin squinted at her in disbelief. While she was eager to get out of the Walker house, she didn't trust Jolene. These were the first semi-kind words Jolene had said to her since she arrived. Actually, they were the *only* nice words she'd heard Jolene say to anybody, all week. On the other hand, what choice did she have?

The Walkers didn't allow Fiona to go farther than the park on her own. Rupert would spot her there. But Jolene was sixteen—they could probably ride the bus somewhere.

Robin nodded. Jolene shouted down the stairs, "Mum? We're going out! For some air! Got our cells!"

Robin shielded her eyes as they stepped outside into the hot, glaring July sun. Jolene spotted the bus turning the corner. "Let's run, or we'll have to wait twenty minutes for another one!" She took off.

Robin ran after her and shouted, "Where are we going?"

Jolene reached the bus and leapt in back as it started moving. "Hand!" she ordered, and yanked Robin aboard. After they flashed their passes, Jolene turned and answered her. "To our favorite hangout, of course." She added, "Do you remember last time we went to the Heath?"

Robin mumbled that she did, while she tried to work out exactly what "the Heath" was, and what Jolene wanted from her now. Jo carried on, oblivious. "I bought you an ice cream, and you dumped it on my head when I refused to take you shopping?"

"Sort of," Robin muttered. "Sorry about that."

Jolene shook her head as the bus rumbled to a stop at a place called Highgate Cemetery. "Fiona and I haven't been to the Heath together since we were tiny. I only go there by myself," she said. She held out a hand.

"I'm Jolene Walker. I believe you are Robin Haggersly. Do you mind telling me where my little sister is?"

OMG. For a moment, Robin thought about just hopping off the bus and making a run for it. What if she just disappeared? Jolene lowered her hand and stared in front of her, saying, "We'll talk when we get off."

Robin spotted the sign for Hampstead as the shops and town homes changed from brownstones to low-slung white cottages with dark wooden beams and pointy roofs made of bundled hay. Grocery stores and pharmacies disappeared in favor of earthy boutiques offering wheatgrass smoothies and natural fiber sweaters. Multiple signs pointed toward the Heath.

Jo rang the bell and rose. Robin reluctantly followed, hopping off the bus onto the pavement and through an alley, before arriving at a pair of colossal wrought-iron gates that opened into a park labeled HAMPSTEAD HEATH.

Even though she was nervous and spooked by Jolene, Robin couldn't help gasping. The Heath was massive and wild. Trees just sprang up where they felt like it, no soccer fields or gardens. Weeds and wildflowers grew in their shade, instead of the usual tidy beds of boxwoods and roses. And rolling green hills—loads of them—dipped and rose again for what seemed like miles, before finally tumbling into the London skyline below. A duck wandered in front of Robin, en route to a silvery pond embroidered with ivy. Sunbathers were everywhere, angling their chairs toward the summer rays, their milky-white complexions turning an unchecked splotchy red. Robin guessed British people didn't get to sit in the sun much.

Jo plonked herself down and patted the grass, commanding Robin to sit. "Like it? This is my favorite place to come and think. Dad used to take us—Fiona and me—here when we were little. We used to fly kites right over there." She pointed to a field. Robin remained standing, frozen by Jolene's way of talking of about "Fiona" as if she wasn't there. Jolene shielded her eyes and scoffed, "Oh, sit down. It's not like I'm calling Scotland Yard. We're at the blooming park."

Robin sat. Jolene started weaving a clover chain. "It was the Eleven Plus that gave you away." She looked into Robin's eyes. "Fi would never, ever, do what you did. No way would she flunk an exam—let alone get expelled—for anyone. Not even Tony. She doesn't have the guts, you see." She grinned. "She's a big girl's blouse."

"A what?" Robin asked.

"She's yellow. Chicken. Whatever you Americans say. You are American, right?" Robin nodded. She had an impulse to defend Fiona, but thought she'd better let Jolene talk. Jo pulled a sheet of wadded-up paper from her back pocket. "Yeah, well, I'd been thinking something was off for a while. You look like Fiona, but you don't move like her—you're always shifting. Your

160

table manners. The incessant questions. The play . . ." She trailed off.

Mention of the play piqued Robin's interest. "What about the play?"

Jolene ignored her question and bluntly stated, "I flunked me O Levels this week."

Robin stared at Jolene in shock. The O Levels were as important to Jo's school career as the Eleven Plus was for Fiona! "What? Why? How do you know?"

"'Cause I didn't take them." Jolene stared at her defiantly. "Was all set to tell Mum and Dad this afternoon about the O Levels, then you do . . . what you did. Fiona has always been little Miss Perfect. Perfect looks, grades, everything. I can't keep up. And since you came, it looked like she was going to be a star onstage, too. So I go, 'All right. Let's see what happens when I go the other direction.' And wouldn't you know it? Fiona's already beaten me there, too. She hasn't just flunked. No," Jolene spat, "she's disqualified, expelled, and a flipping hero for it!" She squinted at Robin, her voice dripping with sarcasm. "Do you have any idea what it's like, keeping up with someone like that?"

Robin nodded and said, "Actually, I do. Sorry, though."

Jolene carried on with her story. "I was all set to rat you out for Facebook. I even printed off the page, just to let Mum and Dad know you aren't some perfect little angel. But I didn't really *read* it the other night. I just

161

saw the posting from that guy and assumed you were talking to boys. Today I saw the messages from Robin Haggersly. Last Sunday week—you tried to tell Mum and Dad who you are, didn't you?"

Robin didn't answer, and Jolene pressed. "Do you have any idea where Fiona is?"

"Japan," Robin whispered.

Jolene's eyes bugged out. "You're joking."

Robin shook her head. Jolene still looked incredulous. "This is a right mess. Japan?" She peered at Robin again. "She all right?" Robin nodded. "Why don't you tell me what happened from the beginning. Can you?"

Robin hesitated. Should she tell Jo about the Wishers? Jo had confessed about her O Levels, so she decided trust deserved trust.

Starting with the swim meet, she confessed everything: who she was, how she'd wished, and everything she knew about the Wishers. She even told Jo about Six Degrees and her strategy to get home. It took so long they were stiff-legged by the time they stood up, their legs imprinted with crisscrossing patterns of grass. "So what do we do?" Robin asked.

Jolene shrugged. "I've no idea. I don't think that Six Degrees idea is going to work. I need to think." She glanced around. The sun had shifted farther west in the sky. "You've got rehearsal, and I've got . . . a little something to do before we leave. Let's head down Lime

Avenue. You'll like that," Jolene added, "as a tourist and all." She skipped off down a winding gravel road canopied by dense trees.

As they picked their way into the woods, the bright afternoon sunlight became thin and filtered. Mansions peeked through the heavy foliage. Jolene stopped at the gates of an enormous house. "Dame Judy Dench lives there. Big movie star. You know her?"

Robin shook her head, while Jo rifled through the shrubs and grabbed a pair of sticks. "I do. She's Mum's friend. She was at my christening." Jo fashioned the sticks into a large, crude fork and used them to scoop up a pile of soft dog poop on the ground. She nodded at the mailbox. "Open it."

Robin stared, horrified. "What? No way!"

"Ugh. Fine. Get out of the way then." Jo pushed the giant turd closer to Robin.

Robin stood her ground and shrieked, "No! Put that down."

Jolene deliberated and finally dropped the sticks and dog poop with a sigh. "So she'd get a little dirty, big deal. She bloody deserves it. Old bat wouldn't write me a recommendation for RADA. Honestly, you're as much fun as Fi."

"What's RADA?" Robin hoped answering the question would change Jo's sour mood.

Jolene pursed her lips and pulled back her shoulders. "Royal Academy of Dramatic Art. Acting school." Jolene's voice grew cold. "You never asked *where* I was when I was supposed to be taking my O Levels. I was at RADA, auditioning. I didn't want Mum and Dad to know. Just as well I didn't tell them, since I won't get in."

She sat down on a boulder. "Me and Fi used to go to all of Dad's plays when we were kids. We made him promise to cast us when we were older. He insisted we had to finish primary school first. Years went by and I forgot about it, but Dad didn't. When I was finishing Year Six, all of a sudden he announced I was starring in *Bridge to Terabithia*. I freaked—thought I'd look stupid—so I refused. That was nearly five years ago and he never brought it up again. Last year, I realized I wanted to act, so I went to Dad again. But he insisted it was Fi's turn now." Her words became bitter. "Fi didn't want to do *Peter Pan*. She told me. But she thought I'd hurt Dad when I refused, so she didn't want to disappoint him again. And she was horrible, she knew she was. So did Dad. He even let me start rehearsing as her—er, as your—understudy, weeks before Fi left. That was the compromise. I thought I was going to get it—Wendy, I mean. After Fi bombed out that Saturday night, she didn't want to go back, and I needed a role for RADA. Then you came along, and all of a sudden, everything's brilliant. For everybody but me, that is." She stood up and started walking again. "Let's take the Tube home."

Robin hustled after her, stunned. "You can't get into the school without a part?"

Jolene laughed bitterly. "It's not required. But it's the best acting school in the world, so it's a bit competitive. They want to know you're good—parts on a professional stage are key. I got through the audition, but they balked when I didn't have any credits. So I tried to force you to quit, over the Facebook thing. I even invited Dame Judy to come opening night. The old bat insisted she had to see me onstage before she could recommend me to the school. Then she found out you were still starring and refused to give me the recommendation."

Robin looked at Jolene with new eyes. She was still petty and mean—the black stripe on Fiona's wall a reminder of what she was capable of doing—but she was also possibly the smartest and boldest person Robin had ever met. Jolene had figured out she wasn't Fiona. Jolene had sacrificed her school exams just to pursue one dream, while Robin had been trying to have it all.

Aaron's words rang in her head: *While you're eyeing someone else's stuff, someone's eyeing yours.* Robin now understood what that meant. She couldn't be mad at Jolene for plotting to steal the show, because, well, she'd tried to do the same thing.

As they passed through the gates to the Heath and onto the main road, Robin made a decision. The words were hard to say, but she forced them out. "Jo, listen. You need the part. And Fiona doesn't want it. I could quit—"

Jolene shook her head. "No. I couldn't."

Robin's voice became shrill. "No, seriously! Just take the part!"

Jolene was equally exasperated. "Fi! Er, Robin, whoever you are." She hung her head. "I'm sixteen! I tried to steal a part from my eleven-year-old sister. Now she's in Japan, and I suppose I'm to blame for that." Tears formed in Jolene's eyes. "I wasn't very nice to her on Saturday, you know. She wished herself away, that's my fault. I don't deserve the part. I won't take it."

A sign pointed to a train station below. Jolene ducked down the steps, and Robin followed. So this was the Tube. Robin had heard the word for the London subway many times. She'd never been on a subway and was dying to ride one.

The underground station was filthy, but incredibly cool: colorful, hexagonal tiles decorated the walls, overlaid with maps and theater posters. Crowds of people pushed and jostled. Jolene shoved her way through so quickly that Robin struggled to keep up. Finally, standing on the platform, Jo stared at the tracks, lost in thought.

Robin watched the ticker above, which assured travelers a train was due in three minutes. It felt like hours. Robin studied the Tube map plastered on the wall just beyond the tracks. One of the stops caught her eye: Wimbledon. The famous tennis tournament wasn't just in England, it was right here, in London! She knew that if her mom was here, she'd be screeching and pointing at it.

A new wave of homesickness washed over her. She craved one of her mom's choking hugs, the kind that usually embarrassed her, the ones her mom delivered when things went horribly wrong. Like now.

A train thundered into the station, obliterating the map on the opposite wall from view and kicking up a sudden wind that blew Robin's hair into her eyes, where it stuck to damp, silent tears. As the train clattered to a halt, Robin picked her hair from her face and turned to Jo to make sure this was the right one. But Jo was gone.

The doors opened and travelers poured out as an announcer's voice boomed, "MIND THE GAP," over and over again. Robin's eyes scoured the platform. Passengers shoved by her, one man using his briefcase as a wedge to fight the crowds. Still no Jo. The doors were starting to close. At the last second, Robin hopped aboard.

Inside, she spotted a smaller version of the Tube map plastered to the wall of the train. She planted herself in a seat beside it, amazed to realize she wasn't scared. A week ago, she would've been terrified. But in the last ten days, she'd traveled thousands of miles alone. A few more miles, with a map at hand, no longer sounded like the challenge it once would've been.

Mrs. Walker was on the phone as Robin walked into the house. "She's just coming through the door now." She hung up. "Thank God," she sighed. "We were so worried. Your sister and Dad are out looking for you now. Why didn't you call?"

"Forgot my phone," Robin said sheepishly. "No big deal."

"You've got rehearsal in about ten minutes."

Robin mumbled, "I need to talk to Dad first. It's been a long day."

Mrs. Walker looked at her sympathetically. "I'm so sorry about the Eleven Plus, love. Not to worry, though—your dad and I are going to speak to the superintendent. We've got an appointment for Tuesday week. We'll get it sorted."

The door slammed. Jolene, flushed from running, stared at Robin a long moment. "You're alive. Good." She stomped upstairs.

Mrs. Walker's expression turned dark. "Jolene! Get back here this minute! Jo!" She followed her older daughter up the stairs.

Seconds later, Mr. Walker came through the door, singing "I Found a Million Dollar Baby (in a Five and Ten Cent Store)."

He spun Robin and dipped her. She giggled. He

168

smiled, his eyes much like her own dad's—full of love. "Don't do that to us again, all right?"

Robin nodded and righted herself; fully aware his scare wasn't over. His baby wasn't home. She hadn't gone missing at a Tube station in London for a few minutes. She'd been gone a whole week. And she was still in faraway Japan.

She wandered over to the desk and flipped on the computer. Rosa, the girl who'd fought to keep an iPod, had posted a message on the Wisher page:

> Robin, it's me, Rosa—the REAL Rosa. I'm home! It feels so good to be ME AGAIN! Liz and I saw your message and we felt really bad. We did like you said—we wished at the same time—to be home. It worked! Oh. If you want to send me your iPod, my address is . . .

Once again, hot, salty tears formed in Robin's eyes. She'd been right! They could go home again, if they wished at the exact same time! Suddenly, the play didn't matter. While she wanted to star in *Peter Pan* and find out for sure if she could act, there would be other chances in her life—her *own* life—to try. What mattered most was going home. And she wanted to be home as soon as possible.

chapter thirteen

Irina Dushaya of Saint Petersburg, Russia

JUST AS ROBIN WAS ABOUT TO CLOSE OUT Facebook, a chat room popped up in the corner of her screen.

Y t?

Alia! Robin was ecstatic.

WHY R U HOME? I THOUGHT U GUYS WERE AT THE BEACH!

Ur family is. I didn't go.

OMG—SO U SAW ABOUT LIZ AND ROSA?

Y.

I HAVE SO MUCH TO TELL U . . . I'VE PRETTY MUCH MESSED UP EVERYTHING.

Robin confessed about finding Fiona. She felt relieved for one whole minute, until she realized she'd have to confess and apologize all over again when Neera got back. While lying is quick and easy in the moment, Robin decided, it's exhausting in the long run. Eventually, you get found out, and if you want to be trusted again, you have to go back to everybody, explain, apologize, and beg forgiveness. And that takes a lot of time.

Minutes went by without a response, while Robin fretted. Had Alia simply walked away from her computer—and Robin's problems—for good? Finally, the familiar ping of a new message came through.

U and I r good. Just don't do it again.

OKAY, DEAL. HAVE 2 GET FIONA 2 WANT 2 WISH. WON'T WISH IF SHE'S IN THE PLAY. AND I GOT HER EXPELLED FROM SCHOOL. AND THEN THERE'S NAOMI. I STILL HAVEN'T FOUND HER. . . .

One thing at a time!

OKAY. THE PLAY. JOLENE WANTS THE PART, BUT WON'T TAKE IT. SHE THINKS SHE'S 2 BLAME 4 FIONA WISHING. WHAT DO I DO?

Get Mr. Walker 2 fire u.

The idea was so simple Robin wondered why she hadn't thought of it before. But how? She suddenly remembered Mrs. Walker's words as she walked through the door—she'd assumed Robin was upset about the Eleven Plus. She could work with that.

I'M GOING 2 TRY THAT NOW. WILL U BE AROUND IN 1 HOUR?

Y.

Robin rose to search for Mr. Walker, but ran quickly back to the computer.

ALIA? WHY DIDN'T U GO 2 THE BEACH WITH MY FAMILY?

Later on that. Go get fired.

Robin found Mr. Walker in the kitchen, sipping his tea and munching on a sandwich. "Ah! There you are, darling. Do you want something to eat before we go?"

"Um, I need to talk to you," Robin responded.

"All right then, here I am." He stuffed the rest of the sandwich in his mouth, wiped his hands on his pants, and chucked his dish in the overloaded sink, starting an avalanche.

Robin took a deep breath. "I got expelled."

"Pah! Not to worry, we'll..."

"No, wait. I'm sure you'll help me get back into school, and maybe I'll get to take the Eleven Plus again. But the thing is, I'll still have to *pass* the Eleven Plus. I wasn't ready for it this time, because I was at rehearsal every night. I want to be prepared." Mr. Walker finally stopped rearranging the dirty dishes and looked at her. Robin met his eyes. "Jo can play Wendy. She wants to, and I want her to. And I need you to fire me."

"Is this about the bed? Told you at the time— wasn't your fault. It's fixed anyway, darling, not to worry. Turned out Bob took a tour of technical school before he became an actor, and he's actually quite a fine welder." Robin shook her head furiously. Mr. Walker grew suspicious. "No? All right. Then I'm guessing your sister has something to do with this."

Robin assured him she didn't, it was simply that her priorities had changed; she needed to take school seriously. Jo starring in the play was the best decision for all involved. She could study, Jo could fulfill her dream, and Mr. Walker could fulfill his. He balked at the idea of "firing" his youngest child, but Robin assured him Jo wouldn't take the part if she quit. He finally kissed her head in surrender and said, "You're growing up, my darling."

Robin beamed at him. "So we're doing this?"

He grinned at her. "I'm looking forward to your performance, actually." He raised his voice, so it would carry up the stairs. "DO YOU MEAN TO TELL ME YOU PULLED THAT FIRE ALARM JUST TO GET OUT OF THE ELEVEN PLUS? I THOUGHT YOU WERE HELPING YOUR FRIEND!"

Robin made her voice whiny. "I did help him! It's just . . . I wasn't ready. . . ."

Mr. Walker raised his eyebrows. "I MADE IT VERY CLEAR, YOUNG LADY—SCHOOL FIRST. YOU KNOW WHAT THAT MEANS. YOU'RE FIRED! JO! GET DOWN HERE!"

"No, wait!" Robin objected, a smile on her face. They heard Jo's feet hit the stairs at a run. It was working!

"Exit, stage right! Don't overdo it!" Mr. Walker whispered. He let go of her hands and Robin took off, emitting a little sniffle just as Jo came storming into the kitchen. Robin sat down outside the door and listened to their argument.

"Dad, if you fire Fiona for getting expelled, you can't hire me," Jo told him flatly. "'Cause I flunked me O Levels."

Mr. Walker exploded. "WHAT?"

Oops. Robin hadn't thought that one through. How could Mr. Walker "fire" Fiona for flunking, only to let her dropout older sister do the part?

Mr. Walker spluttered. "WHY? WHAT THE BLOODY NORA HAS GOTTEN INTO YOU GIRLS?"

Me, Robin thought guiltily. I got into the Walker girls. One of them, at least.

Jo continued patiently, "I didn't take the O Levels. But I had a good reason. . . ."

"LIKE WHAT? YOU WERE SERVING QUEEN AND COUNTRY?"

Robin was about to give up the cause as hopeless when Mrs. Walker swept through the door. "There's been enough shouting," she declared. "Jo, explain yourself and we will have a peaceful family discussion." Mr. Walker started to raise his voice again, but Mrs. Walker put up a hand. "As an actor, I've twenty years training in voice projection. Don't make me use it."

Mr. Walker snuffled in protest while Jo took a deep breath and confessed. "I auditioned for RADA. I made the final callback and I couldn't be at the auditions and my exams at the same time."

Now even Mrs. Walker was spluttering, but Robin could see the smile on her face through the crack in the door. "Jo," she gasped. "My darling! When did this happen? You did this all by yourself? Why didn't you come to us for help? The final auditions? My goodness. And only sixteen!"

Even Mr. Walker was pleased. "That's bloody marvelous, Jo!"

Mrs. Walker now insisted that Jo playing Wendy was probably best for all involved. If Fiona wanted to focus on school, she should. She could have her chance onstage again if she ever changed her mind. Mr. Walker admitted he'd been perhaps a tad ambitious by casting the girls at eleven years old. Jo agreed to go to rehearsal, while Mrs. Walker hustled to the phone, to invite Dame Judy Dench to opening night.

Mr. Walker grinned at Robin. "You knew, didn't you?" Robin shrugged, unwilling to give Jo or herself away. His brow wrinkled. "You know, there's something more going on here," he insisted. "Something . . ." He flapped his hands. "Something big. The kind of stuff stories are made of. You know, 'More things in Heaven and Earth, Horatio,' and all that."

Robin momentarily wondered who Horatio was, and what he'd told Mr. Walker. In any case, he was making her nervous. She froze.

Seeing her reaction, Mr. Walker sniffed. "I believe in stories. I've made my livelihood telling them. So I do hope—at some point soon—SOMEONE feels like telling me the plot." With that, he stalked off. "Jo! Rehearsal! Now!"

Robin watched from the window as Mr. Walker and Jo left for the theater. A pair of arms snaked around her neck from behind, as Mrs. Walker planted a kiss on her cheek and said, "Channel Four's showing *The Chronicles of Narnia* again. I'm going to have a bath, but I thought maybe afterward we could curl up on the divan and watch. What do you say?"

Robin wrinkled her nose. "Don't you think I'm a little old for *Narnia*?"

Mrs. Walker sagged a little bit, but nodded and headed up the stairs. "Suppose you are. Shame, though. Always liked my performance as the Snow Queen."

Oops. Robin kept forgetting Mrs. Walker was an actress. Weird, too, because when she had first met Fiona's mother, it was all she thought about. Robin wondered how many days it had been since she'd started thinking of the older woman as, well, a mom.

Robin called after her. "You know what? I love *Narnia*. When I get my studies done, I'll join you!" Mrs. Walker beamed and headed upstairs toward the bath. A thought occurred to Robin and said to Mrs. Walker, "Hey, um, Mum?" Mrs. Walker turned. "How come you aren't acting this summer?"

Mrs. Walker paused. "I wasn't going to tell you, but since you've quit, I will. There are reviewers at plays, my darling. And they're often cruel. If we Walker women were in the same show—or even rival shows—they'd see it as an opportunity for comparisons, and they wouldn't care if they drove a wedge in our family." She looked lovingly at Robin. "We just wanted you to have your moment in the sun, Fi. So you could know what it feels like to be a star. But there will be other chances." She checked her watch. "I'll just pop into the bath for a while. Let me know if the phone rings."

Robin sat down at the computer and went back to the Wisher page. Another member had joined: Fiona. Naomi Nagata's eyes loomed large in her picture, thanks to the Coke-bottle thickness of her glasses. Robin grinned. Whatever messes she'd made, at least she was sorting them out now. Alia and Fiona were posting back and forth on the wall.

Found it! Naomi's birthday is Thursday. Her passport was in her desk!

The birthday thing again! What was Alia's deal with the birthdays? Robin brushed the question aside and barged in.

UR OUT OF THE PLAY. JO'S IN. JO'S HAPPY, UR DAD IS HAPPY. BUT THERE IS 1 PROBLEM. UR KINDA EXPELLED.

Before Robin could finish typing her explanation, Fiona interrupted.

Can we switch back now?

Robin sighed. DID U JUST READ WHAT I WROTE?

Don't care. Want 2 Go Home.

Alia posted immediately. Fiona. We're all waiting until Tuesday. U agreed.

But Robin promised me she would switch, if I wanted 2. I want 2 switch. I'm not like u guys. I can't do this. I don't know what I'm doing—all the time.

Robin frowned. She really didn't want to wish again, unless she was going home. If she and Fiona wished just so Fiona could get home, Robin would have to be Naomi for four whole days. Still, Fiona had a point—Robin had promised. And she couldn't hold Fiona's body hostage from its rightful owner. Her thoughts churned. Another idea struck her. Robin wrote:

ALIA, I DID PROMISE. MYBE MAKES SENSE. I NEED 2 FIND NAOMI B4 I CAN GO HOME. MIGHT HAVE BETTER CHANCE, IF I WAS NAOMI 4 FEW DAYS.

Alia's answer was instant and adamant. No! Fiona promised me she'd stay put. That's what we're doing.

Fiona chimed in. *But Robin said . . .*

The phone rang right next to Robin. Mrs. Walker called from upstairs.

"Be a love, Fi, and get that for me! I'm waiting on Dame Judy!"

Robin picked it up. "Hello?"

"Robin?"

Robin's jaw dropped as she recognized the voice. "Alia? Why're you calling?"

"You can't." Alia's voice was strangled and upset. "You can't switch with Fiona."

"Shouldn't we be discussing this with Fiona—"

Alia cut her off. "My name isn't Alia. I mean, it is, it's just that—" Alia took a huge breath and the next words rushed out of her mouth. "I lied to you, too, Robin. I was born Irina Dushaya, in Saint Petersburg, Russia. I was a Wisher, but I never got home."

Robin's stomach flip-flopped. "What do you mean?" she choked out.

Alia's voice cracked. "You can only be a Wisher as long as you're eleven. Once you are twelve, or if you're in the body of a girl who turns twelve, wishing doesn't work anymore. You're stuck. I found that out the hard way. Naomi's turning twelve on Thursday in Japan. That's Wednesday for us. Say you become Naomi, but you don't find her before her birthday. Or something goes wrong with the wish. That's IT! You'll be Naomi Nagata for the rest of your life! That's not what you want to do, trust me." Robin could hear sobs on the other end of the phone.

Robin was shocked. So that was why birthdays were so important. Alia had wished, turned twelve, and found out she couldn't wish anymore. She was stuck being Alia Newport the rest of her life. Robin suddenly remembered the story of Alia cutting off her hair in the

179

middle school parking lot, screaming at her mom, "You don't know me!" Now she understood why Alia had screamed—because she wasn't Alia. She was—what was her name again? Something long and Russian.

So why had Alia lied to *her*? Why hadn't she just let Robin wish when she had the chance with Neera? Why had this happened to her? She was just a little girl. They were all just little girls. No one should listen to their wishes, let alone grant them! Fury welled inside her. "And you let me—you just LIED?"

"I'm sorry I didn't tell you! I didn't, because I knew it would scare you and Neera. But your birthdays—yours, Neera's, even Fiona's—were all so far away. I thought we had plenty of time! I also thought if I told you, you'd demand to go home right away. And that meant Neera might not get home at all—" Alia was sobbing so hard she had trouble talking. "I couldn't do that to her. I couldn't do it to anyone. I didn't know about Naomi then. None of us did. Or I would've—"

"But at the time you cared about Neera more than me?" Robin choked.

"No! Listen!"

Being a Wisher was way, way more complicated than Robin had ever guessed. Robin silently did some math. It was Wednesday night. Neera didn't get home until Tuesday. Suddenly, five more days in Fiona's body sounded like a very long time. She wanted to wish and go home, right now. And if she ever got home, she vowed she'd never, ever speak to Alia again.

The other line beeped. "Hang on, Alia," she said, and punched the FLASH button. "Hello?"

"Ah, yes," said a crisp English voice. "Judy Dench calling. Is Petra Walker available, please?"

"One moment." Robin called upstairs, "Uh…Mum? I think it's the call you've been waiting on!"

"Cheers!" Mrs. Walker called. "I'll just get it up here. Go on and hang up, Fi!"

"'Kay," Robin mumbled, and clicked off the phone. She knew she was hanging up on Alia, but she didn't care. Alia deserved it.

Y S T? Where did u guys go?

Fiona was still online.

Robin sat at the computer, tears streaming down her face. What should she say? What should she do? A thousand questions poured into her mind. Like, say Naomi didn't get home by Tuesday. Was Fiona stuck? Would she be Naomi Nagata forever? And if Naomi was in Neera's body, would that mean Neera would be stuck, too? Probably. Neera would never be able to get her own body back.

Fiona pinged again. *What's going ON???*

Should she tell Fiona everything? Yes. Fiona had as much right to the truth as she did. She typed slowly, piecing together her thoughts as she went.

181

WE HAVE 2 FIND NAOMI BY TUESDAY OR WE'RE ALL IN MAJOR TROUBLE.

Robin recounted everything Alia said, as best she could. Fiona cried, but surprisingly dropped all demands to switch right away. Robin finally asked her why.

I'm kinda scared 2 wish at all right now.

Robin typed back. ME 2.

The door slammed and Jolene stalked into the room. "I said I'd do it—the part. But I'm still not convinced about all this."

Robin rolled her eyes. The Walkers, she decided, made an awful lot of demands. And frankly, she had bigger concerns. She thought for a second. "No? Here. Ask your sister." She pushed the keyboard at Jo.

Jolene's eyes bugged at the prospect. "She's there—online? Now?"

Robin pointed at the computer screen. "Here's where we're talking. Here's where you translate from Japanese. I have a lot to tell you, but so does Fiona. And I figure sisters have to take priority."

Jolene began to type, then erased, then typed again. She looked up at Robin in frustration. "I just don't know where to start," she finally admitted.

Before Alia's phone call, Robin would probably have enjoyed watching the elder Walker girl squirm. It would've seemed like righteous payback for a week of torture. But now the stakes were too high. If their plans didn't work out, Jo might never see her sister again. A vision of Sophie popped in her head, her tow-white hair and green eyes peeping out from underneath Pudding, her beloved blanket. Would she ever see Sophie again? She'd give anything to talk to her little sister. With that in mind, Robin suggested, "Why don't you start with 'I'm sorry and I love you'?"

Jo wrinkled her nose. "She's my sister, not my grandmother."

Robin put her hands on her hips, and Jo surrendered. "All right! All right! I'll write it!" She typed. An answer came within moments. Jo smothered a laugh.

"What's it say?"

"She says I've gone all toady."

Robin smiled. "I didn't know Fiona had a sense of humor."

Jolene tilted her head. "Really? She's actually quite witty." Her fingers flew across the keyboard. Robin leaned in to read again, but Jo blocked her.

"Look, um, can I just have a moment, here, please? This is somewhat private."

Robin colored. "Okay. Sorry." She wandered away from the computer, missing her own family so much it hurt. And she was too tired in body and spirit to wait for Jolene to finish with the computer. She headed upstairs.

In the stillness of the bedroom, Robin thought about the consequences of not finding Naomi. Consequences.

She hated the word. She even hated how it sounded—con-se-quen-ces—lots of hard sounds, all put together. The word was like a rock knocked off a cliff that kept smashing other rocks on its way to the ground.

What would she do if they didn't find Naomi by Tuesday? Or what if they did find her, but Naomi didn't want to go home? Would Robin switch with Fiona? Sacrifice herself, just to save a girl she'd never met? At the same time, could she really refuse? What about Neera?

A voice startled her out of her panic. "You should've told me. Tuesday?" Jo stepped into the room and slid onto the beanbag chair. Robin nodded but said nothing. "What do we do?" Jo asked. "Any ideas?"

"I've got to find Naomi. Somehow," Robin whispered.

They both stared at the ceiling until they heard Mr. and Mrs. Walker clomping up the stairs to bed. Robin instantly felt guilty—she'd forgotten about watching Narnia with Mrs. Walker. Then again, maybe Narnia wasn't such a good idea. Narnia was about four kids walking into another world, a dangerous one. Robin had already walked into another world herself. And now she was scared she'd never get home.

chapter fourteen
Naomi Nagata of Kyoto, Japan

THURSDAY MORNING, ROBIN STUMBLED DOWN
to breakfast, more exhausted than she'd ever felt after
a late night's rehearsal. She'd struggled to get to sleep,
then woken repeatedly from nightmares in which her
face, body, and location kept changing like a slide show.

In the kitchen, the magazine *Time Out* was neatly
folded and waiting for her on the table. Her mouth
dropped in surprise.

WALKER STUMBLES
By Cherie Cherie

*Director Nigel Walker caught flack
months ago for casting Fiona, his neophyte
eleven-year-old daughter, in the starring role
in the Haymarket Production of* Peter Pan.
Time Out *learned yesterday Walker has now
fired Fiona, due to her abrupt expulsion from
primary school. But ever the upstart, Walker*

shocked producers again when he cast his eldest child, sixteen-year-old Jolene, in the lead role. Sibling rivalry takes on a whole new meaning, and the Walkers' personal drama threatens to upstage their West End production.

It had never occurred to Robin that newspapers would be interested in the fact she got expelled from school and fired from the play. Yesterday, their stinging words might have hurt. But that was yesterday. Robin shoved the magazine in the trash as the doorbell rang. She headed to the front hall and swung the door wide. Rupert stared at her in disbelief, as though she was an alien. He waved a copy of *Time Out*.

"Have you gone balmy, Fi?" He ran his fingers through his hair. "First the Eleven Plus thing, for that—that tosser," he spat. "Now this! Why did you do it? And why haven't you answered my texts?" He folded his arms like an indignant parent.

Robin wasn't sure what "balmy" meant, but she guessed it was some kind of crazy. Fine. She could live with that. But calling Tony a "tosser"—whatever that was—was too much.

She folded her arms and stared back—hard. She noticed Rupert's ears were too big—he kept his curly hair long just to cover up how they stuck out. Plus, his blue eyes were small and beady. Apart from his looks, she couldn't think of any reason to like him. She still remembered how he'd treated the old American couple. How he'd treated Tony at school. Fiona didn't like this guy, and suddenly Robin didn't, either. She placed her hands defiantly on her hips.

"Are you allergic to yellow jackets, Rupert?"

"What's THAT got to do with anything?" he demanded. She continued staring at him, until he admitted, "No. Why?"

"Because I am. And you saw me trying to duck one, and you did nothing. Tony helped me, even though he was allergic, too. He's a hero. And you, you ..." She searched for a way to describe just how little she thought of him. Jolene's words flashed in her head. "You're a BIG ... GIRL'S ... BLOUSE." She slammed the door for effect, only to remember something else. She yanked it open again. "And just for your information, I happen to LOVE Americans!" She slammed it a second time.

Despite her desperate situation, Robin couldn't suppress a small grin. So what if he was the most popular boy at school? Big whoop. She didn't need to waste ANY time on a boy who was afraid of a tiny little bug.

The self-doubt she'd felt when Jason dumped her back in North Carolina was gone. Jason was as cowardly as Rupert—he'd been too scared to call and break up with her, so he'd just shown up with Jasmine at the swim conference. Robin deserved more. So did Fiona. All girls did.

"Who was that?" Mrs. Walker demanded from the stairs.

"Loserville," Robin answered.

Mrs. Walker obviously wasn't listening. "I've got tea with Dame Judy later this afternoon. Do you want to tag along?"

"Oh. Uhh . . . I was planning on studying all day, if that's all right?"

Mrs. Walker beamed at her. "That's the spirit, Fi! Power of positive thinking. Study for the Eleven Plus and you will sit the Eleven Plus. We've got six weeks summer vacation to make that happen. Right you are, then."

Robin opened her books at the desk and waited until Mrs. Walker left. A split second after the door shut, she turned on the computer. A private message was waiting for her on Facebook.

Robin,
I'm so sorry. I really wanted to help, to fix things, for you and Neera. And truthfully, I was hoping that maybe in helping you, I could also help myself. That was wrong. You may not want my help anymore, and I deserve that. But I owe you my story, just in case. I promise it will be the truth.

Like you, I wished on my eleventh birthday. I ended up in Indonesia. I didn't like Indonesia, so I wished again, not knowing if it would work a second time. I just wished over and over again, until I guess someone else was wishing, too. This time I ended up in Canada, as a girl named Shannon Piefer. I loved being Shannon—she was pretty, problem-free, and Canada was a breeze compared to my home in Russia. (As much as I love my home, it's a hard place to live.) I ignored emails and phone calls from every Wisher who tried to contact me, because I didn't want to go home. After a little while, I didn't even feel like Irina Dushaya in Shannon's body anymore. I just felt like Shannon. As it turned out, Shannon had problems, too, just like you, me, and every other Wisher out there. I didn't like having problems. I wished again and became Alia Newport. I thought I could go on forever, changing bodies whenever things got hard.

But I wished myself into Alia's body on her twelfth birthday. A few weeks later, I decided that I would like to spend my own twelfth birthday in my own body. I figured it would be like a vacation—I could leave again whenever I wanted. So I finally answered Alia's emails— she was in my body. We thought it would be easy, and we wished. Nothing happened. Then we started wishing like we were in a marathon. Nothing happened then or since, even though we still wish every birthday. Alia lives my life, and I live hers.

My home in Russia and my family are nothing like yours, but now there's nothing I wouldn't trade to see them again. I can understand why you want to go home so much. I hope my story helps you get there.

Now about you. You have to realize there are Wishers out there who are like I was, girls who think they don't want to go home. Neera's not like that, so I figured you were both safest staying put until we found everybody. I thought we only had to find Fiona, so I didn't tell you about turning twelve. But I had no right to make that decision for either of you.

If you want my help, you've got it. I won't make decisions for you, and I won't lie to you ever again.

The Real Irina Dushaya

Robin didn't cry. She'd cried too much yesterday. But all the feelings that came with crying—anxiety, misery, loneliness—rushed through her.

There were Wishers out there who didn't want to go home. And there were more Wishers who didn't know wishing ends at twelve. Any one of them might wish on Tuesday and wreck all of Robin's plans to get home. Robin didn't want to believe Alia, or forgive her, either. She couldn't, because if she did, she'd have to accept that what Alia was saying was true, and that was scary.

Empathy arrived last, hitting Robin like a wave, washing away all the anger she so desperately wanted to keep. Poor Irina and poor Alia, living out the rest of their lives as somebody else. In her heart, Robin knew Alia had been punished enough.

It was insanely early in the United States, but Alia was online. Robin's response to Alia's letter was blunt.

I NEED HELP FINDING NAOMI. RIGHT NOW. & UNTIL WE FIND HER.

Robin! Seriously? U've got it! Again—I'm so sorry.

WHY'RE U AWAKE?

Do u honestly think I could've slept???

GUESS NOT. DOES NEERA KNOW? ABOUT THE 12 RULE?

No. She doesn't. I didn't tell her because she was upset enough already.

ABOUT WHAT?

U kept disappearing. She said u could go home whenever you wanted 2—all u had 2 do was ask. She couldn't do that—she had to wait on a snail mail. So every time u disappeared, she worried u wouldn't come back and she'd be all alone.

Robin had never really thought about it that way. No wonder Neera was so upset! What a crummy friend she'd been! She shook herself into action.

IF NAOMI'S IN NEERA'S BODY, NEERA'S AT RISK, ISN'T SHE? I MEAN, IF NAOMI CAN'T GET BACK TO HER BODY THEN—

Robin couldn't bear to finish the thought. Alia responded with a single letter.

Y.

WAS THINKING . . . U DIDN'T KNOW ABOUT 12 RULE WHEN U WISHED. MAYBE NAOMI DOESN'T, EITHER. WE HAVE 2 FIND HER & TELL HER. CAN U JOIN THE SIX DEGREES FACEBOOK EXPERIMENT? ON FB HOME PAGE? WE'VE GOT TO FIND SOMEONE WHO LIVES IN GAWA, INDIA. SEE IF THEY CAN PASS ON A MSG.

Robin explained her idea and they set to work.

Despite no school and no rehearsal, Robin was dazed by how fast Thursday and Friday passed. She and Alia worked tirelessly, using the Six Degrees Experiment and an atlas to try and find someone in or near Gawa, India, who could and would contact one Neera Gupta. Even Jolene helped in between the double rehearsals Mr. Walker called every day. But they had no luck. The language barrier, combined with the unusual request to contact an eleven-year-old girl, was simply too strange.

Mrs. Walker noticed Robin's depression and mistakenly assumed it was because of what had happened at school and with the play. On Friday afternoon, she switched off the computer and said, "Get dressed. We're going shopping."

Robin protested. "But I have—"

Mrs. Walker interrupted. "You HAVE to get dressed. No arguments."

Reluctantly, Robin dressed and accompanied Mrs. Walker on the Tube to Sloane Square. When the escalator took them to the surface, Mrs. Walker took her hand and led her to a street called King's Road.

In any other circumstances, Robin would've flipped out at this opportunity. King's Road was similar to what she imagined shopping on Rodeo Drive in Beverly Hills would be like. Boutique stores with the names of famous designers on their awnings lined the boulevard. Inside the stores were leather sofas and chairs, where customers could comfortably sit and regard the mannequins dressed in haute couture, then whisper their size to the gorgeous models that worked there. The correct size was retrieved from the back and delivered to a changing room. Mrs. Walker strolled easily between the stores, shaking her head at some offerings—too old for Fiona, too skimpy, too last year—and giggled and smirked at others. Occasionally, she'd glance at her downcast daughter, hoping Fiona would forget her troubles and join in the fun.

But Robin just couldn't get in the mood. Even a sighting of bad-girl movie star Lindsay Lohan, lounging on a sofa in one of the boutiques, failed to pique her interest. As Friday afternoon became Friday evening, Robin tapped a dress with disinterest and begged Mrs. Walker to take her home.

She was running out of time to get in touch with Naomi.

But Mrs. Walker's motherly ministrations that afternoon had an effect. In Robin's dream that night, Mrs. Walker was hugging her when she suddenly turned into Robin's mom. Robin tearfully asked her what to do. Then Aaron appeared, and she asked him the same thing. When she woke up, ideas started pouring out of her mind. She couldn't wait to put them in action.

Saturday morning, Robin posted a message in capital letters on the wall.

NEED ALL THE HELP WE CAN GET. CALLING ALL WISHERS! FIONA, Y T?

An answer pinged in the chat room window.

I am!

DORI?

No answer.

GUESS DORI'S NOT AROUND. HERE'S WHAT WE'RE GOING 2 DO. FIONA, PLAY DETECTIVE. READ EMAIL—NAOMI'S, HER PARENTS, EVERYBODY. SEE IF SHE'S MADE CONTACT. CHECK SNAIL MAIL, PLUS CELL & HOME PHONES FOR MSGS. IF U

DON'T FIND ANYTHING, CALL HER FRIENDS. MYBE THEY'VE HEARD FROM SOMEONE CLAIMING 2 BE NAOMI.

K. What r u going to do?

SEARCH ONLINE—NAOMI MIGHT HAVE ANOTHER EMAIL ADDRESS WE DON'T KNOW ABOUT. ALSO CHECK OUT MORE WEB SITES. I FOUND DORI THAT WAY. MYBE FIND NAOMI 2—IF I LOOK HARDER.

A few hours later, Alia joined the hunt. Robin assigned her a task.

ALIA—REMEMBER THAT FAMILY TREE PROJECT U & AARON DID 4 SCHOOL?

Yeah . . .

THAT'S WHAT UR DOING 2DAY. EXCEPT THIS IS A WISHER FAMILY TREE. DO U STILL KNOW SOME WISHERS? CAN U GET IN TOUCH?

I can try.

TRY. EACH MIGHT KNOW AT LEAST 1 MORE WISHER. I KNOW—WAS 3 YRS AGO—BUT 1 OF THEM MIGHT KNOW A WISHER FR 2 YEARS AGO. MYBE A WISHER FR 2 YRS AGO KNOWS A WISHER FR LAST YEAR, & MYBE ONE OF THEM KNOWS SOMEONE WISHING NOW. SOMEBODY MIGHT KNOW NAOMI. GET LIZ AND ROSA TO HELP IF U CAN.

I'm on it!!!

At one o'clock in London, Liz's and Rosa's alarm clocks were ringing in Ohio and Brazil. They both saw the message on the wall and joined the hunt.

Even Jolene borrowed a laptop and sifted through Web sites during her rehearsal breaks.

Robin split her time between doing her own research and directing Wisher cyber traffic. Fiona pinged constantly with questions, while Alia worked frantically, contacting every Wisher she'd ever known or been. By mid-afternoon, six former Wishers had friended them on Facebook, bolstering all their hopes. But none had ever heard of Naomi Nagata.

Taking a break from Google, Robin opened a chat room with Alia.

HOW COME UR HOME, ANYWAY? WHY AREN'T U AT THE BEACH WITH MY FAMILY?

Aaron and I broke up.

WHY?

Robin, maybe ur gonna get angry at me, but I told him about u. He didn't believe me or Neera.

AND HE BROKE UP WITH YOU???

By five o'clock London time, Fiona finally had to give up and say good night. It was already two o'clock in the morning in Kyoto and although she wanted to keep going, she was too tired to come up with any new ideas. By seven o'clock, Robin's eyes were also blurry from staring at the screen. She'd emailed at least four dozen Naomi Nagatas. She'd already heard back from several—polite emails that stated she must have the wrong address. She had to admit she was disappointed; she'd been positively convinced that today would be the day.

A little while later, Jolene barreled through the door. "I've got it," she announced. Robin rubbed her eyes.

"Did you know if you get some really contagious disease, like smallpox or flesh-eating virus—even if you're just exposed to it—they quarantine you?"

Robin had no idea where this was going.

Jo continued, "Guess what they give you while you're stuck in quarantine? A computer!" She clapped her hands. "That's what's supposed to keep you occupied. You talk to your friends and family on the Internet! And it just so happens my mate Jamie works at the World Health Organization—"

Robin cut her off. "We're not getting Naomi quarantined. At least, not yet."

"Just hear me out. Jamie's willing to come up with a story how Neera Gupta of Gawa, India, might've been in contact with someone with an infectious disease. He'll call the Indian Center for Disease Control, they'll round her up. Bang. She's somewhere with Internet access. Robin, I know it's not ideal, but—"

Robin interrupted her with a flat no.

"You've been trying it your way all day and it hasn't worked," Jo argued. "Fi's almost out of time."

Samantha De Groot's gorgeous face popped up on the wall.

Hellooo!!! Back from the city! Was awesome

compared 2 this dump. Much 2 tell! Who r all these new people?

Jolene regarded the post with interest. "Is that another one? A Wisher?" Jo peered at the picture on the Facebook wall. "Samantha De Groot. Blimey. South Africa?"

Robin was so tired. She said, "Her real name's Dori Simpson, and she's from Hawaii."

Jolene was fascinated. "Cool! Always wanted to go there."

"She doesn't," Robin grumbled. "She doesn't ever want to go home." Robin had stronger, more negative feelings about Dori, in light of Alia's story. But she needed help—Jo was right, they were nowhere. She resisted her impulse to tell Dori to go home and typed back.

HELLO, DORI. ROBIN HERE. ALIA 2. WE'VE BEEN LOOKING 4 U. TRYING 2 FIND MORE WISHERS. NEERA IS STILL AT THE BEACH. LIZ AND ROSA HAVE GONE HOME—

Dori posted before she'd even finished.

Robin! How r u? BTW, no worries about sending Rosa yr iPod. I sent her new one 2day. De Groots are loaded, no biggie.

THANKS, DORI, THAT WAS NICE! ME, NOT 2 GOOD. TRYING 2 FIND NAOMI NAGATA.

Why do you want to get in touch with Naomi?

Robin leaned forward in her chair.

DORI, DO YOU KNOW HER?

Well, nvr met her, obviously, but online I know her. She was in my network.

Robin was stunned. Dori posted again.

Ur not thinking of going home r u, Robin?

Alia chimed in. Dori, any idea how we can get in touch with Naomi?

Wait. How'd the interview go, Robin? Are you a big star now? When does the play open?

Robin had forgotten to tell Dori about quitting the play. She started to type an answer, detailing how she'd been fired, but Jolene erased it. "Don't tell her you've quit."

Robin was incredulous. "What? Why not?"

Jolene rolled her eyes. "She's got something you want. She knows Naomi. And you've got something she wants—stories of fame. Commerce first, confessions later."

"I don't want to lie to her," Robin said.

"Give over." Jo sat down and started typing herself.

HELLO, DORI, THIS IS JOLENE. ROBIN HAD 2 GO, BIG DAY COMING UP. I'LL HAPPILY FILL U IN, BUT DO U HAPPEN TO HAVE A WAY TO GET IN TOUCH WITH NAOMI?

Email. Not her regular one at home. 2 many Wishers use those. She started another one.

So Robin had been right! Naomi did have another email!

"How does she use it, though?" Robin wondered aloud. Jolene typed back.

I DON'T THINK NAOMI HAS A COMPUTER WHERE SHE IS. HOW DOES SHE READ THESE EMAILS?

Duh! Internet café! This one girl I know talks 2 Naomi every week. Both use secret emails & schedule times to talk. They're really hypersensitive tho. Don't have Naomi's email but do have her friend's. She could pass on a msg. Maybe.

OKAY. CAN I HAVE THAT GIRL'S ADDRESS, PLEASE?

What happened 2 Robin? Who r u, BTW?

I AM ROBIN'S NEW PERSONAL ASSISTANT. ROBIN'S GOING TO BE A BIG STAR, SO SHE NEEDS HER SLEEP. SHE TOLD ME ABOUT WISHING AND ASKED ME TO FILL IN. SHE'S REALLY BUSY— DOUBLE REHEARSALS TOMORROW, LUNCH W/ JONAS BROTHERS & AN AUDITION FOR A SPIELBERG FILM. NOW, DO U HAVE THAT EMAIL ADDRESS FOR NAOMI'S FRIEND?

"What are you DOING?" Robin demanded. Dori's response was immediate.

Cool! Hang on a sec. Will get address.

Jolene grinned. "Getting you what you wanted. She wants to live vicariously through you, so I'm just keeping you interesting. Anyway, what difference is it going to make?" Robin shook her head, sure there was something wrong, but she was too tired to figure it out.

Here it is: sdegroot@transvaalnetwork.co.sa. Oh, BTW. She doesn't like me so don't tell her u got this from me. Is Robin planning on going home? What about the play? And the Jonas Brothers?

Jolene typed back.

Cheers, Dori. Signing off now.

I want to hear all about the Jonas Bros. tomorrow! Gnight.

"Sorted!" Jolene declared. "Going to bed now."

Alia popped up in the chat window.

Robin, that's an email address for Dori's Wisher—Samantha De Groot. Dori told us she didn't know Samantha. Now it looks like she's been talking to Samantha all along at this secret email address. Why would she lie? Something is wrong!!!

Robin sighed. The same thought had occurred to her.

SO DORI LIED ABOUT HER WISHER. WE'VE ALL LIED. I UNDERSTAND WHY SHE LIED—SHE DIDN'T WANT 2 GO HOME. I HAVE NO IDEA WHY SHE'S TELLING THE TRUTH NOW. MAYBE BECAUSE WE'RE ALL PLANNING ON GOING HOME, DORI'S DECIDED SHE WANTS TO GO HOME 2. ANYWAY, I'M SURE IT'S NO BIGGIE. I'LL JUST WRITE TO THIS SAMANTHA GIRL AND SEE WHAT SHE SAYS.

Robin fidgeted over what to say to Samantha De Groot. How was she supposed to write a letter to Samantha, when she didn't know whose body Samantha was in, or even where she was? She really should've asked Dori a few more questions.

But Dori had gone to bed, and Robin didn't want to lose another day.

To: sdegroot@transvaalnetwork.co.sa
Fr: fwalker@comcast.co.uk
You don't know me, but I'm a Wisher like you. I used to be Robin Haggersly of Concord, North Carolina. Right now I'm Fiona Walker of London, and you're my last hope.

It's urgent I find Naomi Nagata. I think she's in the body of my friend Neera Gupta in India.

I just found out that wishing stops working on your 12th birthday. I don't know if Naomi knows that, and her birthday is on Thursday. So Tuesday here—Wednesday in Japan—is the last time Naomi, Neera (who's in my body), Fiona (who's in Naomi's), and I can all get home. As in EVER.

We're planning to wish ourselves home that day, but we've got to make sure Naomi knows, or it's all ruined. I've heard you're in touch with her. Can you please send me her email address? My email is above and my number in the UK is 44–01–171–787–0809. FYI, we've also started a Wisher Network on Facebook if you want to check it out. Just look up Fiona's name and I'll add you as a friend.

chapter fifteen

Samantha De Groot of Kimberley, South Africa

SUNDAY MORNING, AN EMAIL WAS WAITING
in Fiona's inbox.

> **To: fwalker@comcast.co.uk**
> **Fr: sdegroot@transvaalnetwork.co.sa**
> We didn't know wishing stops at 12. Naomi
> is in India and she said to tell you she wants
> to wish. She will be by a computer Tuesday, 4
> p.m., London time. She will contact you. This
> is the ONLY time she can be by a computer,
> so have your wish plan ready.
> Samantha
> P.S. I have looked at your Facebook site.
> I don't want to be on your Wisher Network.
> Don't email me at this address again, either.
> I MEAN IT.

Robin read the message with Jo leaning over
her shoulder, sipping her morning tea. Jo's brow
furrowed at Samantha's "I MEAN IT."

"What's got her knickers in a twist?" Jo asked.

Robin felt a flush coming to her cheeks, too. Why was this girl so rude? Why wouldn't she pass along Naomi's secret email address? What was the big deal? But worries about the mysterious Samantha De Groot were quickly replaced by a more exciting realization. "I don't know, and I don't care. I'm going home!" Robin said as the reality sunk in. She'd done it! She'd made contact with Naomi, and she was going home! They all were! On Tuesday! She wanted to cry with happiness.

"You're going home, Fiona's coming home. Thank God," Jo said. "So, suddenly you've got a couple of free days. I have rehearsal at eleven, but afterward, I can take you somewhere. What do you want to do? See some sights? Buckingham Palace? Or the Tower! Torture chambers!" Jo grinned.

Robin thought. "Actually, there is one place I need you to take me, before you go to rehearsal."

They stomped through a surprise rainstorm and rapped on the door of a brownstone row house much like the Walkers' house. Tony answered, and Robin beamed at him.

"Hi! I called, but they said you were still at the hospital. I just wanted to say thanks—about the bee, I mean. I'm sorry I didn't come by sooner, but I didn't know where you lived." Jolene elbowed her, while Tony's face scrunched in confusion. Robin realized her mistake. Duh! Fiona Walker had been coming to this home since she was a toddler. "Er, I mean . . ."

He waved off her explanation. "It's all right. Do you want to come in?"

"Cheers," Jo said as she barged through. She nearly tripped on a heap of camping equipment in the middle of the floor. "Blimey. Going somewhere?"

Tony nodded. "We all are. Wimbledon."

Robin's eyes widened in surprise. "As in the tennis match? For real?"

"Oh, you're not"—Jolene wrinkled her nose— "camping for tickets?"

Tony gestured out the window. "It was supposed to be the men's final today. My parents had tickets, but it's pouring. So now we have to camp."

Robin was lost. "Why does that mean you need to camp?"

Jolene explained, "There are no rain dates at Wimbledon. If the Sunday final gets rained out, we have People's Monday. All the seats are up for grabs. You have to camp out in the queue though. All night in the rain."

Robin was thunderstruck. "How many seats are there?"

Tony took over. "Fifteen thousand. So our chances are pretty good, if we get moving. We're off as soon as my parents get back from the store."

Jolene scoffed. "Can't wait to tease your sister.

Bet she just LOVES this idea. She in?" Tony nodded toward the stairs. Jo continued, "I'll just go catch up with her." She elbowed Robin and gave her a meaningful look.

Alone with Tony, Robin suddenly felt horribly awkward. "Your hand's better," she finally blurted out. "I'm glad. I'm sorry I caused you to—"

"No, I'm sorry you got expelled. I'm the one who needs to—"

"But I'm the one who—"

Tony held up both hands to stop her. "We both said thanks, and we both said sorry. There." He offered her a hand and she shook it. But Robin was sure Tony deserved more—she'd treated him horribly, and he'd still saved her, and he'd suffered for it, too. As she leaned in for a hug, he turned his face toward hers and gave her a hesitant peck on the lips. Seeing her surprise, he quickly pulled away.

"Sorry, I guess I thought—" He wrung his hands, embarrassed.

"No, it's okay," she insisted. "I just never—" She stopped herself from saying "kissed a boy before." Too embarrassing! But she couldn't come up with words. She felt all flubbly inside. Tingling, in a nice way. The soft dampness lingered on her lips.

If there was a boy to give her a first kiss, Robin was sure this was the boy. But she was leaving, and Fiona was coming home. Whatever Robin said or did now affected her. "Look," she said shyly. "I'm just . . . not ready, you know? Friends?"

Relief flooded Tony's face as Jo returned. "Got to get back, Fi," Jo said. "Best of luck at Wimbledon, Tony," she called. "Ta for now, feel better, all right?"

"Bye," Robin said shyly. He smiled back at her as the door closed.

Robin splashed a hundred paces in the rain before cornering Jolene. "Remember how you said you could take me to see some tourist stuff?" Jo nodded as Robin took a deep breath. "Well, I've thought of something. I'd really like to go to Wimbledon."

Jo snorted. "Get bloody serious! That's going to be a madhouse."

Robin met her eyes. "I am serious. I have to go to Wimbledon."

Jo realized Robin wasn't kidding. "What on earth for? You haven't watched the tournament coverage since you got here. Do you even know who's playing?"

"No," Robin admitted. "That's not why I'm going."

"Well then, why are you going? I'm not sitting all night in some bloody queue, in the rain, simply to watch the most boring tournament on earth."

Robin groped for an explanation. "You aren't the only who wasn't very nice last week. My mum—I mean my mom—" Just talking out loud about her mother brought a lump to her throat. "My mom loves Wimbledon. She's crazy about it, actually. When we were little, she came up with Wimbledon Day. We'd all dress up in tennis outfits, eat strawberries and cream, and watch the final together. Or at least we did, until I said it was stupid. I thought if I went—"

Jo interrupted. "Very touching. Robin, even if we took pictures, you couldn't show her. And we probably wouldn't even get in!"

Robin nodded. "I know. But I've got to try. You said yourself I have some time on my hands. I can't talk to Naomi or Neera until Tuesday. I haven't done a single thing for my family since I got here. I can go to Wimbledon, if you'll take me."

Jo groaned. "Oh, I suppose I owe you this much. Fine. We're doing back-to-back run-throughs and should be done around four o'clock. While I'm there, you get the camping gear out. It's in the attic."

"Thank you!" Robin threw her arms around Jo.

"All right, all right, don't gob all over me! Pack carefully, with every creature comfort I might possibly need. And I need A LOT."

Robin eagerly agreed. Wimbledon! They walked another half a block, lost in their own thoughts, before Jolene turned to her with an impish grin. "So! Fancy Tony, do you?" Robin shrieked and ran.

At five o'clock that afternoon, Robin and the Walker family emerged from Southfields Tube station and joined the streaming mass of humanity moving south.

Mrs. Walker called out, "Nigel! Grab the cooler, would you? Jo, give us a hand!"

Mr. and Mrs. Walker had balked at the girls camping out at Wimbledon alone. They argued vehemently to drop the entire plan, but the girls presented a united front. Jo reminded her parents that journalists kept calling their home, wanting to talk to Fiona Walker, the "primary school dropout." Wimbledon would be a chance for her to get away from her troubles. At that, Mr. Walker declared, "We'll all go. After rehearsal."

Robin was mesmerized by the volume of people. Everyone was sloshing through the muddy streets of Wimbledon, overloaded with backpacks, tents, and deck chairs. News crews stood at every corner. Reporters interviewed hopeful campers about the rarity of a "People's Monday," and the campers responded in more languages than Robin knew existed. Some had bought tickets a year ago. They'd planned their trips and flown thousands of miles simply to attend Wimbledon. Those campers complained loudly. Others were grinning adventurers who admitted they'd heard about People's Monday on TV. They'd come on a whim, hoping to attend Wimbledon this one time, just to say they'd been.

Robin loved every minute. Even the air smelled like hopes and dreams.

A steward waved them toward a line that went as

far as Robin could see. He barked, "Honor the queue! Queue cards will be distributed shortly."

Mr. Walker and Robin stepped into the line, shifting and standing on tiptoe to examine how far they were from the front. Mrs. Walker and Jo followed, dumping down their bags and grunting as they unfolded deck chairs. Jo indifferently flipped through a magazine before demanding, "How long will we have to wait?"

Mr. Walker shrugged. "I've no idea. Never done this."

At a crack of thunder, Jo held out her hand expectantly toward Robin. "Brolly, please." Robin rifled through her backpack, looking for the umbrella. As the first raindrops started to fall, she flashed her empty hands at Jo, "Oops."

Jolene stared, incredulous. "You've got to be joking." With an exaggerated sigh, she plonked her magazine on her head.

As evening became night, the rain let up, replaced by a dew-laden fog. Tents popped up all over Wimbledon golf course and tiny barbecue fires flickered, their glows reminding Robin of the fireflies that lit the backyard of her North Carolina home.

"Who wants a sausage?" Mr. Walker called out as he rolled the hot dogs with his fingers on the small hibachi grill he'd purchased at a nearby grocery store. They all raised their hands, starving. Mr. Walker passed out plates and licked his fingers. "Mmm!!! Years since I did this!"

Wimbeldon stewards did not expect everyone to stand in line all night. Instead, they'd handed out queue cards—wristbands that designated their place in line—after a three-hour wait in the pouring rain and directed everyone to the golf course to camp. The entire would-be Wimbledon audience was staked out here, their tents so close together their poles crisscrossed. Robin guessed that from up above, the golf course probably looked like a gigantic game of tic-tac-toe. They would be woken promptly at 6:30 a.m., at which point they would present their queue card and resume their place in line until all 15,000 seats were sold out.

Jolene shuffled a deck of cards. "Game of Snap?" Robin raised her eyebrows to signal Jo she didn't know how to play. Jo whispered, "I think you call it War."

After losing three hands in a row, Robin looked expectantly at Jo. "What?" Jo demanded.

"I'm waiting for my jellied eel."

Mr. Walker burst out laughing, while Jo gathered up the cards. "I believe we're done with jellied eel, aren't we?"

Even though the sky was now clear and brilliant with stars, Mr. and Mrs. Walker said good night and trundled off to the tent, while Jolene and Robin stretched out on the wet grass and stared at the sky.

"What're you thinking about?" Jo asked lazily.

"My brother, Aaron. I wish he could see me here. I mean—me, not Fiona. Remember when you asked me about living with someone who's just about perfect?"

"He's your Fi, is he?"

Robin nodded.

"It's not his fault, you know," Jo argued.

"I know," Robin admitted. "And he's actually pretty cool. It's just that this," she gestured to Fiona's face and body, "happened to me. For once, something amazing happened to me, not Aaron, and he doesn't even believe it. Alia told him. She even showed him the Facebook page, but he didn't believe her."

"Yeah, but Robin, come on. It's a bit hard to believe."

"And then there's the play. I mean, I'm glad you're doing the part—I really am—because even if it was me going onstage in two days, it wouldn't be me. It would be Fiona. But I was good at it, you know? Not Aaron—me. For once. But Aaron's not going to believe that, either."

Jo spluttered, "It hardly matters, Robin!"

Robin's brow furrowed in confusion. "What do you mean?"

Jolene gaped at her. "Robin, c'mon! Being a Wisher isn't what makes you special. Nor is being a good actress. It's you. You're the single, most sympathetic person I've ever met in my life. You take on everybody's problems, and you try to help. Do you think I do that? Does your brother? I bet not. Most of us have enough of our own problems. Can't be bothered with someone else's."

Robin grumbled. "I'd still like him to believe me. About the wishing, I mean. He broke up with Alia over it."

Jolene let out an exasperated sigh. "And there you go again!"

As the first rays of dawn peeped over the golf course, the bleary-eyed Walker family packed up their camping gear and stored it with the stewards. Robin insisted on keeping a large backpack with her as they took their places in line. Hours later, they stood at the majestic wrought-iron gates of Wimbledon. A triumphant Jolene waved tickets high in the air. "We're in!"

Robin's eyes glowed as she walked through the gates, recognizing all the places her mom had pointed out over the years on television—Aorangi Pavilion, Court 2—the famous "Graveyard of Champions"—and Henman Hill.

"We're off this way," Mrs. Walker declared, pointing.

"Wait!" Robin cried. She pulled the backpack from her shoulder. "There's something I need you to do."

"I feel like a right nutter," Mr. Walker declared, regarding his tennis whites, sweater vest, and the cap that sat at a jaunty angle on his head. "Anyone would think I'm expecting one of the finalists to ask me if I wouldn't mind filling in."

Jolene popped her head out of the bathroom, scowling. "Say anything. I dare you." With that she stepped out into the sun, sporting a too-short tennis dress.

Robin smiled at them. She felt a little silly herself, wearing Fiona's pleated white skirt and polo shirt, but she wasn't giving in. No way. The moment she'd seen their tickets, she'd yanked out her heavy backpack and started distributing tennis outfits she'd found tucked away in the attic, next to the camping gear. As far as she was concerned, she'd done her best by the Walkers for two weeks. Now it was time to do something for the Haggerslys. Robin guessed her own parents must've felt silly for years, dressing up in tennis togs to watch the match on TV. They'd done it for her and Aaron and Sophie. The least she could do was return the favor. And that meant playing dress-up at Wimbledon, per family tradition.

Mrs. Walker alone seemed pleased with her white skirt and polo shirt. "I'd forgotten I had this," she said admiringly. "Makes my legs look great."

"Your legs are great, my darling," Mr. Walker affirmed. "Shall we?" Mr. and Mrs. Walker linked arms and headed to Centre Court, while Jolene tied a sweater around her waist.

"Maybe we should try for advance tickets next

year," Mr. Walker proposed as he gestured them into their last-row seats, high above the backcourt as an announcer welcomed them all to the Wimbledon Men's Singles Final. The announcer proceeded to read off a long, long, LONG list of rules of how to behave as audience members at Wimbledon: no signs, no yelling, no waving, no fist-pumping. . . . Robin wondered why he didn't just say, "You can clap and that's it." Bored, she scooped up strawberries and cream and tried to memorize every last detail of the stadium: the lush lawn scuffled bare at the serving lines, the hats and gloves of the stodgy, whispering people in the box seats. Above and behind her was a half-built retractable green awning. Next year, in the event of rain, this awning would cover Centre Court. This would be the last "People's Monday" ever. And she was here to see it.

The music swelled. "Ah, the Queen!" Mr. Walker announced. "Up you get!"

The Royal Family? The REAL ONE? Robin knew they always came to Wimbledon—her mom had eagerly pointed them out on TV every year—but it was weird to contemplate sitting in the same stadium as a queen. Curious, she craned her neck for a look. She pointed. "Is that Prince William?"

Jolene swatted her hand down as though she done something rude. "Yes! Don't be such a tourist! You'll meet them tomorrow night. Or at least, Her Royal Highness."

"What?" Robin stared at her in amazement.

"Oh. Did I forget to mention they're coming to opening night?"

Robin screeched in excitement, momentarily forgetting the long list of Wimbledon rules. She was luckily muffled by the thunderous applause that welcomed the finalists as they walked onto the court. Robin joined the cheers, enthralled. Wimbledon was exciting after all, she decided. Who knew?

During the first set, one of the players sent a high volley into the stands. Jolene grabbed at it and missed. When the man next to Jo caught it, the cameras zoomed in on him. Jo stared at him for a moment and leaned over to Robin. "Is your brother watching this?"

Robin nodded. "He never misses it."

She held out a hand. "It's the end of the set. Come with me."

Five minutes later, they hustled back to their seats, Robin now cloaked in Jolene's big cardigan, sweating profusely. "I'm boiling! And what if the ball doesn't come up here again? What if he doesn't see it?" Robin asked.

"If it's meant to happen, it'll happen," Jolene barked. "But we'll never know if you let that sweater fall open. We'll get tossed. Keep it closed."

Late in the third set, a volley beelined for their heads. Jolene said, "Now!" yanking the sweater from Robin's back as they stood. The sweater fell away and

Robin lifted her arms to catch the ball. The man next to Jolene caught it again, but this time Jo jabbed an elbow into his gut, and he dropped it with a grunt. Robin scooped it up as Jolene shouted, "Cameras are on you, wave it high!" Impatient, she grabbed Robin's wrist and lifted the ball triumphantly into the air. A TV cameraman zoomed in on them, filming the girls and the words Jolene had scrawled in big letters on Robin's polo shirt:

BELIEVE IT
AARON HAGGERSLY

chapter sixteen

Robin Haggersly wishes

ROBIN OPENED HER EYES. IT WAS TUESDAY!
Naomi was going to call! Neera was coming back! And
they were all going to wish themselves home! Robin
sprang out of bed and ran to the computer. Alia had left
her a message late Monday night.

U r crazy. But thank you.

Robin smiled. Alia had seen the Wimbledon Men's
Final. She wondered if Aaron had, too. But it was three
o'clock in the morning in North Carolina—too early to
talk to anyone.

In the kitchen, while Mrs. Walker stacked the
dishes, Jo grabbed the toast Robin had just buttered
and stuffed it into her mouth. "So where are you off to
today, Mum? Salon? Prep for HRH tonight?"

"Should do, shouldn't we? I'll just call Bibi and
see if he can squeeze us in," Mrs. Walker was already
texting away on her cell.

"Us?" Robin repeated.

Mrs. Walker looked surprised. "I assumed you'd
want to come with me, Fi."

"I do, it's just that umm, I mean . . ." As irresistible as a makeover trip sounded, Robin felt like a visitor who needed to get packed for her trip home. "I'm waiting on a call," she blurted out.

"So take your cell," Mrs. Walker argued, looking up from her phone. "There. Bibi can take us at one o'clock. Let's do something REALLY outlandish!" She clapped her hands and looked at Robin. "What do you say?"

Robin raised her eyebrows at Jo, pleading for help. Jo smirked. "I think Fi means she's waiting on the kind of call that requires PRIVACY." Seeing Mrs. Walker's confusion, Jo mouthed the word "Tony."

Mrs. Walker shook her head and grumbled. "I don't know why she thinks Tony's going to be interested after she scribbled another boy's name on her clothes. Right strange that. Guess I'm on my own, then. We have to be at the theater by seven, Fi. That means we have to leave here by six thirty. So be ready," she instructed, and wandered upstairs.

Jolene toyed with her toast. "So what time are you guys doing this?"

"What? The Wish? Don't know yet. That's why I have to stay here. But I will try to see you in the play, don't worry."

Jolene mumbled something incoherent.

"What's that?"

Jo shifted uncomfortably and raised her voice slightly. "Is there any way you'll ever come back? To visit, I mean?"

Robin stared at Jo, a huge smile coming to her face. "You're going to miss me!" she said accusingly.

Jolene glared. "You're deliberately making this awkward! But yes. I'm going to miss you."

Robin ran over and hugged her. "Toady!" she declared. "I'll miss you, too. Maybe you can come and visit me in the States."

Jolene tilted her head. "Oh! I like the sound of that. Can we go to New York? No! Wait. Los Angeles! Rodeo Drive!" Robin giggled, realizing Jo had absolutely no sense of just how far those cities were from her home. Oblivious, Jo wandered off, making plans for her future trip.

Mr. Walker and Jo left the house at nine and Mrs. Walker soon after them. Robin ambled around the house, waiting for four o'clock, when Naomi Nagata would make contact. Jo's good-bye had made her realize she'd never be in this house again as a member of the Walker family. As impatient as she was to hug her own family, the truth was she'd fallen in love with another one while she'd been waiting for that to happen.

The faded, peeling Walker house wasn't much to look at, but now it felt familiar and comfortable. And the Walkers themselves seemed to light the house with their glow, better than bright paints or lush fabrics ever could. She thought of Mr. Walker, singing his songs and regarding her with those gentle gray eyes. He'd made her feel loved from the moment she arrived, working with her on the part of Wendy, then dropping his work to fulfill her Wimbledon whim. Mrs. Walker was lovable, too, with her constant demands for peace and justice. Jo made Robin feel respected, grown up. Ever since she'd learned about Wishers, Jo had relied on Robin's leadership to bring her sister home.

Was she still ordinary Robin Haggersly? Robin wasn't sure. She felt different, but how much of that was tied to being Robin Haggersly the Wisher? What would happen when she went home?

At eleven a.m., Alia popped up online.

Can't believe u did that.

LOL! DO U THINK AARON SAW?

If he didn't, someone will tell him. Let's get organized. What time do u want 2 wish?

LET'S SEE. NAOMI TURNS 12 AT 3 P.M. TOMORROW, LONDON TIME. SO I THINK BEST 2 WISH 2NITE, JUST 2 B SAFE. IN CASE THERE R ANY MIX-UPS.

But we can't even tell Naomi when 2 wish until 4 your time.

I KNOW! & THERE'S NEERA—MY MOM SOMETIMES STOPS AT ANTIQUES STORES ON THE WAY HOME FROM THE BEACH. MAY NOT BE BACK UNTIL 3 OR 4 O'CLOCK YOUR TIME. THIS IS CUTTING IT CLOSE. BUT WHAT ABOUT 10 P.M., LONDON TIME? THAT'S 5 IN NC. OH. 1 PROBLEM.

What's that?

I'LL BE AT THE PLAY. WILL HAVE FI'S CELL, BUT WON'T BE BY A COMPUTER FOR THE WISH.

That IS a problem! Robin, this wish is 2 important 2 rely on everything going 2 plan. & Neera and I can't call ur cell, remember? What if we have 2 contact u???

Alia was right. Robin, Fiona, Neera, and Naomi were on four different time zones in four different countries. They had to synchronize their wish perfectly, because they wouldn't have a second chance. Because across the international dateline in Japan, it would be Thursday and Naomi would turn twelve. What if someone needed to make a last-minute change to the wish plan? Who could contact Robin?

There was no getting out of the play—none of the Walkers would allow Fiona to miss meeting the Queen or seeing Jolene in her debut. Robin had simply planned to have Fiona's cell phone with her, just in case, but she'd forgotten Alia and Neera couldn't call it. Jo had had the answer why: Fiona, like most kids, didn't have an international-calling feature on her cell phone. Robin couldn't make or receive calls from Alia and Neera.

She needed a go-between for their wish. Alia and Neera were out. Jo would be onstage. Fiona and Naomi would still be speaking foreign languages, so even if they could call, Robin wouldn't be able to understand them. Samantha De Groot wouldn't help—she'd made that pretty clear in her email. Liz and Rosa had disappeared back into their own lives. That left one possibility. Robin checked her Facebook chat room window.

Y T?

Hello, Robin!!! How were the Jonas Brothers? Tell me ALL!!!

Robin shook her head. Jolene shouldn't have told Dori tales.

DORI, R U GOING 2 BE BY A COMPUTER 2 NIGHT?

Duh! These De Groots never go anywhere! Really boring here, compared 2 U. U know, it's not like I thought here. Samantha's parents sit around this stupid farm all the time and talk on their cell phones. Meanwhile there's nobody for me 2 hang out with! Most of the time I can only talk to the maids and they're even more boring than Sam's parents. So I just sit here, straightening my hair and doing my makeup, just in case somebody feels like taking me someplace. (U wouldn't know it from my FB pic, but Samantha's not really all that pretty—she just works at it. 4 one thing, her hair is insanely curly. If I don't flat iron for like an hour every day, I look like I stuck my finger in the electrical socket.)

As Dori continued to complain online, Robin grew increasingly aggravated. She thought about reminding Dori that a week ago, she'd vowed she'd be Samantha De Groot forever. Now all Dori wanted to do was insult Samantha, as well as everybody Samantha knew and loved. But Robin had a more urgent problem.

DO ME A FAVOR? TEXT 44-01-171-555-1212 RIGHT NOW?

Wait a sec.

Fiona's cell beeped. Robin threw a triumphant fist in the air. It worked! She'd thought it might—Dori had gone on and on about how rich the De Groots were. An international-calling plan was probably no big deal to them.

WORKS! YAY! DORI—I'M GOING HOME 2 NIGHT. WE ALL ARE—ME, NEERA, FIONA, AND NAOMI, 2.

Why???

XPLAIN LATER. WISH IS AT 10 P.M. LONDON TIME. I'LL BE AT THE PLAY—THE QUEEN IS COMING. NO ONE IN OUR GROUP CAN CALL MY CELL XCEPT U. CAN U STAY BY COMPUTER IN CASE SOMETHING GOES WRONG?

Y. Still think ur crazy—the Queen? 4 real? And you still haven't told me about the Jonas Bros.

DORI—GOTTA GO. VERY IMPORTANT. R U 100% SURE U WILL BE HOME?

Count on me. Bye.

Robin breathed a sigh of relief and went back to Alia.

ALIA? I SORTED IT OUT. DORI'S UR CONTACT.

R u sure? I mean, Dori? For real?

WHAT CHOICE DO WE HAVE? HER PHONE WRKS—WE TESTED IT.

K. I'll FB Fiona info.

The phone rang so often the day passed quickly by. Most were reporters, eager for comments about opening night. But in the midst of the chaos, Tony Newsome phoned asking if Fiona was going to be at the play. Robin assured him she was and asked why, just as her home number in North Carolina beeped in.

"Tony, I have to go! It's a call from the U.S.!" Robin clicked over, concerned. "Hello?"

"Robin? Robin?!! Is that you, sweetie"?

Why was Aaron calling her "sweetie"? He'd never called her "sweetie" in his life. "I'm fine, Aaron—"

"Oh my God!"

Robin heard the phone hit the floor. What was his problem? Then she remembered—the accent! He'd never heard it before. She grinned, thinking just how weird this must be for him. She heard him pick up the phone.

"Okay, I just freaked out a bit. Now listen to me, I'm gonna get this all sorted out. Don't cry. Neera says you guys can wish tonight. I think—"

Robin interrupted him. "Aaron."

"—that if we just—"

"AARON!"

He paused. Robin made her voice as authoritative and mature as she could. "I've got this. You don't have to do anything." A thought occurred to her, and she made her voice stern. "Except apologize to Alia! You were a real jerk for doing that."

"I know! I'm sorry! It was just—you're my sister. I'm supposed to—" He was so upset his voice cracked. Robin couldn't believe it. She thought about teasing him, but decided she'd better not. Just hearing his voice made her feel closer to home.

"It's okay," Robin continued. "I've already set everything up. Well, almost. I'm still waiting on this Naomi girl. Anyway, if everything goes as planned, I'll be home for dinner. Hey! Did you see me? At Wimbledon? Oh, and Aaron! You know that British guy in—ugh, can't remember the name of the movie. The one about the car? You know, the guy with the beard? Yeah! I was in a play with him! A professional one! He's really nice. And guess what?! It's opening night tonight, and the Queen is coming! I'm going to meet her!"

"Are you serious?"

"Yes! And that's not all. . . ." Robin started telling her brother about her incredible two weeks. When she'd finally finished, she heard him suck in a breath.

"This is amazing! I can't even believe you want to come home!"

"Aaron, it's not like you think. I mean, it is pretty cool and all, but it's scary being Fiona, too. And Fiona wants to get home. She doesn't want to be in the play, and . . ."

"I don't mean being Fiona. Or even being in England. I mean you. You're amazing. Robin, think about it. You were in the same situation as everybody else, but you contacted Neera, you started the Facebook thing, you even found all the other girls—Naomi, Fiona—and you don't even speak the same language. Alia says no Wisher's ever done what you've done."

This time it was Robin who nearly dropped the phone. Aaron thought she was amazing? The most she'd ever gotten from her big brother was a "sure, you did good," and he only offered that when he was put on the spot by her parents.

Her silence was so long Aaron finally asked, "Robin, you still there?"

"Umm, yeah."

Just then, Mrs. Walker stumbled through the door, her arms loaded with packages. Robin stared—her curling red locks were piled high on her head, spiking at the top in all directions. She looked like a water fountain.

"Give us a hand, would you, Fi darling?"

"'Kay." She returned to the phone. "Look, Aaron, I have to go. See you tonight!"

Aaron responded quickly. "Okay. Hey, Robin? Be careful, sis. Love you."

"You too! Bye!" She hung up and ran to help Mrs. Walker.

"Thanks, luv. That was that Aaron boy again? I thought you were interested in Tony!" She sighed loudly. "I can't keep up."

Robin checked the clock behind Mrs. Walker: four p.m. Naomi! She grabbed the packages—she needed to hustle Mrs. Walker out of the room. She talked as she headed for the stairs, hoping Mrs. Walker would follow. "I love your hair!"

Mrs. Walker smiled and patted her head nervously. "Do you? I really wasn't sure about it." She shifted to review herself in the mirror, before turning and regarding Robin from head to toe. "Have you even showered?" she demanded.

"Um, no, but I have one more call to make. . . ."

"Ten minutes," Mrs. Walker said sternly. "Then it's off to get ready." She headed upstairs, while Robin raced to the computer screen. An unfamiliar chat room window was already open. Robin typed hesitantly.

NAOMI?

Yes.

Robin breathed a sigh of relief as she typed.

HOW R U?

No questions. 2 hard 2 translate. What time wish?

TONIGHT AT 10 P.M. LONDON TIME.

Okay, bye.

Considering how hard she'd worked to find Naomi, Robin had expected the conversation to be a little longer, and a little warmer. But on the other hand, what did she care? She'd be Robin Haggersly tonight, and she'd never have to think of Naomi Nagata or Samantha De Groot ever again. She turned back to the computer.

FIONA, NEERA! TALKED 2 NAOMI. ALL SET FOR 10 P.M. LONDON TIME. DORI IS OUR GO-BETWEEN IF ANYTHING GOES WRONG. EVERYBODY READY?

Fiona answered first: Y!!!!!!

Neera's response followed a minute later: *Hello and good-bye! We're going home!!!! Can't believe u did all this while I was away. Alia says if u hadn't, Naomi would've turned 12 and I would be—*

Robin realized what Neera was about to say and cut her off.

DON'T EVEN GO THERE. I OWED U. U DID SO MUCH WHILE I WAS BUSY BEING FIONA. I KEPT THINGS FROM U. I'M SORRY I SCARED U.

It's okay.

Robin could hear Mrs. Walker heading to the top of the stairs. She was out of time. She typed furiously.

NEERA, I WILL MISS YOU HORRIBLY. PLEASE WRITE ME. OR BETTER YET, GET A COMPUTER SO WE CAN KEEP TALKING WHEN UR HOME!

Neera's last message popped up. Will miss u 2.

Mrs. Walker's voice boomed down. "Fiona Walker! You need a shower, and I insist on doing your hair. So head up these stairs right now, please!"

Minutes after Robin and Mrs. Walker raced out the door, the phone rang and rang. An email popped up in Fiona's mailbox, but Robin never saw it.

To: fwalker@comcast.co.uk
Fr: alianewport@carolina.rr.com
Re: URGENT
DON'T TRUST DORI, NO MATTER WHAT
SHE SAYS!!!! I TALKED TO SAMANTHA DE
GROOT.

At seven o'clock in the evening, Robin stepped out of
the car as all the billboard lights of Piccadilly were
just flickering on. It seemed as if the city itself was
as impatient for night as Robin was. The Haymarket
Theatre was decked in opening-night splendor with
flowers and velvet ropes lining the entrance. Best
of all was the red carpet, paving the way to Jolene's
stardom.

Robin stepped onto the carpet and looked at herself
again in the reflection of the car window. She'd never
owned anything like the shimmering silver baby-doll
dress she and Mrs. Walker had picked out on King's
Road. Her own mom would've said it was "way too
grown-up." Robin took a little twirl. The fabric glittered
and sparkled, the feather-light folds lifting and floating.
Mrs. Walker had curled Fiona's cropped brunette hair
into perfect ringlets for the occasion.

Funny, Robin realized. Fiona Walker looked ready
for a magazine cover, but Robin no longer pictured
herself as the model. Fiona's face was beautiful, but it
wasn't hers. She missed her own little heart-shaped

face, light brown hair, and brown eyes. She could barely wait to see it staring back at her in the mirror.

Aaron saying she was "amazing" had made her proud. She'd never really given any thought to what she'd achieved as a Wisher. She'd only chalked up what she'd accomplished—and what she'd failed at—as Fiona. As it turned out, she did have a souvenir she could to take with her when she left Fiona and England behind. She now knew that Robin Haggersly wasn't ordinary after all.

A photographer's flash startled her out of her thoughts. He indifferently snapped a few photos before turning his attention to the curb once again, obviously looking for any sign of the Royal Family's motorcade.

Mrs. Walker was already at the door of the theater. "Coming, Fi?" Robin turned to hustle after her, then stopped, realizing she needed to take a last look around at London.

"I'll be there in a sec," she said, and wandered to the edge of the red carpet. She would miss England, she realized with surprise. She loved the old buildings, and the statues that paid tribute to people who'd lived hundreds of years before she was born. She loved walking on streets that had been trodden on by kings and queens. She loved the traditions, like Wimbledon.

She loved the people, too. Not just the Walkers. She thought of Tony, Stef, Captain Hook—so many people.

There was something besides their accents that bound them together. Something in the way they behaved made them all unmistakably English. What was it? In a heartbeat Robin knew. It was their instinct for calm. The British didn't get freaked out, or at least, they didn't show it the way Americans did. She'd always assumed that people were just people—some you liked and some you didn't and it didn't matter where they were from. But she realized now that every person— English, American, Indian, Russian, or Japanese— carries the best parts of their home inside themselves.

The slanting sun cast a long shadow of Fiona across the carpet, as if to announce the dark she'd been waiting for was on its way. She silently said good-bye to England and headed inside. Weird, she thought, to go inside a building you knew you'd never walk out of.

Stef waved at her from the double doors between the foyer and the theater. "There you are! Your dad just sent me to find you. He wants you to join the cast onstage—the Royals are on their way." Robin nodded and fell into step without a word. She felt suddenly awkward, an outsider. Stef scoffed and snaked an arm around Robin's neck, tightening into a choke hold. "Don't you know how to say hello? How you been, anyway? Missed you."

Robin said hello and giggled as they made their way down the aisle to the stage.

"Found her," Stef announced.

Another pang of longing greeted Robin as they stepped onstage. She missed being part of this happy zoo. Mr. Walker was gesticulating at the technicians as they guided the fly system into place. The stage manager barked orders as the lighting cues flashed various colors and spots in quick succession. Dark-suited strangers roamed the stage with dogs—Robin guessed they were like the secret service agents back home, checking out the area and making sure it was safe for the Queen. Off to one side, Captain Hook was teaching the costumed cast an appropriate bow for a queen.

"One hand on your torso, like so," he ordered. "Now lower your head slowly—eyes down, William," he said accusingly. Hook spotted Robin and swept over in his usual grand way. He gave her a hug. "So good to see you, my darling, we've missed you. So sorry about what happened." Other cast members, still bowing, suddenly peered up and spotted her. A general chorus of "Fi" rang out as they surrounded her, talking eagerly, until a stagehand ran down the aisle. "They're here!"

Mr. Walker clapped his hands. "Right, here we go, receiving-line places, please." He hooked Robin's arm in his own. "You stay with me."

While the cast bickered in loud whispers, poking and elbowing one another, a familiar blue dress caught Robin's eye. Dressed as Wendy, Jolene Walker quietly took her place in the receiving line and stole a glance at Robin. Her eyes were surprisingly shy and seemed to ask, *Is this okay?* Robin instantly decided to ignore the pang of longing she felt for the costume she'd worn so proudly herself and planted a beaming smile on her face in response. Jo smiled back, her relief visible. She pointed at Robin's outfit and mouthed, "Snazzy."

The doors at the back of the auditorium opened. Robin felt her eyes grow wide with amazement. The Royal entering the Haymarket Theater was definitely NOT the Queen.

"Ah, not the Queen," Mr. Walker whispered in confirmation. "Our young Prince, actually."

A surge of excitement rippled through Robin, as Prince William made his way to the stage. Tall and blond, he spoke softly and smiled often as he walked down the receiving line, wishing them all the best in their production. He took Jo's hand warmly and whispered a greeting, but his eyes were searching for something. Or someone. Robin planted her eyes firmly on the floor, as his shadow stopped in front of her.

"Your Highness." Mr. Walker's bow was grand, compared to Robin's quick flick of a curtsy. "Many thanks for your gracious attendance of our little play." She felt the Prince's eyes on her, and he whispered something to one of the dark-suited men. The dark-suited man stared at her, too, as they flipped through a clipboard. Robin turned red with embarrassment. She felt like an exhibit at the zoo. Prince William addressed

Mr. Walker. "Is this your younger daughter? Miss Fiona Walker?"

Huh?

Mr. Walker's brow wrinkled. He looked as confused as Robin was, but he nodded and introduced Fiona. The Prince extended his hand. "How do you do, Miss Walker? I'm William. I understand you know a boy named Tony Newsome?"

His hand felt soft and cool as Robin shook it, trying to overcome her shock. Why was he asking for her? And how did Tony know Prince William? She struggled to answer, knowing she must look like a dork. But, well, the Prince of England was holding her hand!

"I . . . I . . . ," she stammered. "Yes?"

"Ah, good! So I have the right one!" There was a general gurgle of pleasure from his assistants and guards. He continued, "Mr. Newsome is the young cousin of my—Kate. Do you know her?"

Kate? As in the Prince's . . . ? Tony was related to her? "I, I—" Robin recovered. "Tony and I went to school together, but I got expelled!" she admitted.

Prince William nodded sympathetically. "Yes, so I heard. Mr. Newsome was very upset about what happened to you. He said you saved his life. So he called his cousin today and asked if I could help. She called me. I think you are a very brave girl. I thought we might take a picture together." He looked around. "Can we do that? Do we have time?" The dark-suited men shuffled, and one of them whispered to the Prince. He smiled again. "Wonderful. Come on, then," he said, taking her hand. "Let's go take a picture."

Robin was confused. "Wh . . . Where are we going?"

"Outside. You see, there are plenty of cameras out there. And the photographers all work for newspapers. And," he added with a deliciously perfect smile, "I have a feeling they'll be happy to take our picture. Maybe that will help with your situation."

The pang of loss Robin felt when she'd first walked into the Haymarket evaporated as she stood on the red carpet, decked in a beautiful dress, and holding the hand of Prince William. Cameras flashed wildly as he solemnly declared her a hero and shook her hand. The moment was quickly over, but the flush of excitement stayed with her. She beamed as she hugged Mr. Walker and Jo backstage for the last time and whispered good-bye in Jo's ear. She was positively radiant as she took her seat in the audience next to Mrs. Walker, especially when she overheard the excited whispers of fellow audience members identifying her as "that girl, she was the one with Prince William." She clapped and cheered as the music started and the curtain lifted. She proudly watched Jo's performance as Wendy, all the while holding Fiona's cell phone, keeping a close eye on the time.

Close to nine p.m. she felt Fiona's cell phone

vibrate. She turned slightly in her seat, away from Mrs. Walker as she read the text message:

WISH AT 9:45. 10 IS 2 LATE. DORI

Too late? Too late for what? Robin squirmed in her seat, uncomfortable. This didn't make sense, but she didn't have any idea what to do. She struggled to focus on the play, but questions poured into her head, as she tried to imagine why the time had been changed. When the lights came up for intermission, she raced into the lobby, Dori's cell number already on her screen.

But Dori's cell phone rang and rang, finally defaulting to voice mail. A small whimper escaped Robin's lips, as Mrs. Walker spotted her and rushed over. "What's wrong, darling? Is it the play? Is it too much?" Robin shook her head and checked the time— too late. Even if she told Mrs. Walker she was ill now, they'd never make it back to the Walker house in time to call Neera. What if she didn't wish at 9:45 and missed her chance to get home? What if she messed up everyone's chances? Why wasn't Dori answering her cell? Had her battery died?

"I'm fine, I just need some water," Robin croaked.

"Right away, my love." Mrs. Walker hurried off, and Robin punched Dori's cell number again. She continued to punch it, even as Mrs. Walker returned and the lights flashed for them to retake their seats. "Seems to be going well," Mrs. Walker mused.

Robin nodded in agreement. "Jo's the best part."

As Act Two ticked slowly by, Robin prayed for another message from Dori, righting everything to the originally scheduled 10:00 time. But no messages came. Her time in England dwindled. 9:42. 9:43. 9:44. Onstage, Wendy prepared to walk the plank, Robin prepared to wish. She had to try. For herself and Neera. And Fiona. And Naomi.

9:45. Robin closed her eyes and whispered the words, "I wish I was me."

chapter seventeen

Robin Haggersly of
Concord, North Carolina

MUFFLED VOICES PENETRATED THE DARKNESS.

Somewhere a boy asked loudly, "WHAT HAPPENED?"

Yeah, Robin thought, *that's what I'd like to know, too*. She drew a breath, but the air felt thick and soupy going down, like a milk shake through a straw. She tried to open her eyes, but they wanted to stay closed. She wanted to sleep—that was it. Sleep would feel so good right now. Maybe just a few minutes. Then she'd get up.

A girl answered, her voice hesitant. "Oh my God, she fainted. It's normal, if you . . ." The girl paused.

"WHAT? IF YOU WHAT?" the boy demanded.

Wait a minute. Robin knew his voice.

The girl sucked in a breath before answering, "If you wish."

That's right! She'd wished!

"But it's only—" he argued in a hushed voice.

Robin still couldn't open her eyes, but she finally managed to croak out a dry, rasping, "Aaron?"

She felt his breath as he leaned over her. "I'm right here. Um, Robin? Is it you? Can you open your eyes? You want me to call Mom?"

At the mention of her mother, Robin's eyes popped open and she did a quick inventory of the room: ceiling fan above, built-in bookcases to the left, her dad's *The Complete Sherlock Holmes* prominently on display. Computers on antique library tables to the right, each glowing with Facebook pages, and three gigantic windows, from which afternoon sunlight filtered through the stately elm trees of North Union Street, Concord, North Carolina, USA. She was in the library of her own home. AS IN HOME!!!

Robin glanced at her hands—short and stubby, fingernails that could use a clean. She didn't care. They were her own hands and therefore absolutely wonderful. "I'm me again," she said incredulously. "Feels so WEIRD! I mean, good, but—" Robin balked again at the sound of her own voice. "I sound so weird, too!" Her voice was high and flutelike again, no more throaty Fiona. Her American accent sounded a little strange, too, after two weeks in England. She'd never really thought of herself as having an accent before. Huh. It was kind of cool—made her feel like an international traveler.

Aaron knelt behind her, trying to pick up her shoulders. "Welcome home. C'mon, try to sit up," he ordered. Alia offered Robin a hand.

"I got it, I got it!" Robin protested, and picked herself up to a sitting position.

Alia grinned, her green eyes twinkling with happiness. "It's awesome to see you again, Robin."

On instinct, Robin threw her arms around Alia's neck and hugged her. They'd been through so much that even a hug just didn't seem to cover it. They rocked back and forth, a sob of relief escaping from Alia's throat. Aaron lifted his hands, in an exaggerated expression of incredulity. "What, don't I get a hug?"

Robin smiled, surprised. "You've never wanted a hug from me!" She plucked herself off Alia and hugged her big brother. "Toady!"

"Huh?" Aaron asked.

Robin shook her head and said, "Never mind."

"Oh my God, what time is it?" Alia said as she lifted herself up and headed to the computer. She spun back to Aaron. "It's five minutes after," she said hesitantly. "Do you think we should call—"

Robin interrupted, excited. "You think anyone else has posted that they're home yet?" She scrambled, but reeled, still feeling the aftereffects of the wish.

"Whoa there, sis. Take it easy." Aaron grabbed her arm and pulled her up. Robin plonked herself into the other desk chair.

"Thanks," she said, impressed that her big brother was helping her.

The Wisher page was still on-screen, and Robin

Haggersly was signed in. Robin was about to write a message on the Wisher wall while Alia bounced nervously up and down. "Robin, I've got something to tell you before you write—"

"What?" Robin answered, rejoicing again at the sound of her own voice, as she typed merrily on the wall.

THIS IS ME!!!!!! AS IN ROBIN HAGGERSLY! AND I'M HOME!!!!

"There," Robin said proudly.

Alia looked at Aaron and Aaron shrugged in response. "There's nothing we can do now," he insisted. "We might as well just see who turns up."

"What're you guys talking about?" Robin demanded, but kept her eyes glued to the screen. "Hey, look! Naomi's online! She's home!!"

"What?" Alia and Aaron crowded around the screen to see the post Naomi had written and translated herself.

Whoa, dizzy. But I'm home! Thank you, Robin! And Happy birthday to me! I'm twelve. No more wishing! Ever! Bye for now.

Aaron folded his arms and looked triumphantly at Alia. "There. No reason to panic. Naomi's home. No one's stuck forever, and besides, we can't reach anyone else. Fiona's still at the show, and Neera doesn't have a computer." He smiled at her. "Don't worry. You did good. You both did. It's okay. Now. Can we get on with the Welcome Home party?"

Robin beamed. "You organized a party for me?"

Aaron tilted his head from side to side, weighing his answer. "Obviously, we couldn't hold an official party for you," he said. "But it'll feel like one, I promise." Placing his arm around Robin's shoulder, he guided her to the library door. Alia hesitated, but Aaron mouthed something at her. She smiled and followed them out.

I guess they're back together, Robin thought happily, although she was a little grossed out. Why would someone as great as Alia want to kiss Aaron? Major yuck.

A giant ball of chocolate fur came barreling down the hall toward her. Robin screeched with pleasure, "KITTY! Kitty, whoa!" Kitty barked in response, jumping and spinning in circles, almost knocking her down. "Down!" Robin ordered, already feeling more like her old self. Kitty sat, impatiently wagging her tail and licking Robin's hand. Robin threw her arms around her dog and hugged her. "I missed you so much!"

"I guess somebody knows *you*," Aaron said. "She growled at Neera. Like, all the time."

Standing in the foyer of her family home, Robin looked around. School pictures of her and her siblings were artfully angled on the tiger oak mantel, everything gleaming from fresh polish. Robin realized what a relief it was to look around a room and recognize the people in the pictures. In the hall, mail on the sideboard was opened, sorted, and organized into neat little piles. Only the wooden floors were dirty, thanks to Kitty's dusty new pawprints. Robin smiled at them. Usually she resented cleaning up after her dog, but tonight, she was so grateful to live in a house with a pet again she'd happily get on her hands and knees with a sponge. She'd never seen any house so beautiful in all her life. She wanted to drink in the sight of every room and kiss every last member of her family.

She caught a glimpse of herself in the mirror over the mantel and couldn't resist taking a closer look. She giggled when she realized she'd have to stand on tiptoes to see her whole face. She was short again! And it was GREAT!

The black eye had healed—her brown eyes loomed large in the mirror. She'd never noticed before, but she actually had little hazel flecks in her brown eyes that made the color sparkle. But her hair! Robin ran her fingers through her cropped locks and turned to the side. Actually, not bad! While it was different, and she'd never have had the courage to cut it that short on purpose, it was sort of flattering and definitely fashionable, like the blunt cuts she'd seen on Fiona's classmates in London.

Alia grinned. "Neera absolutely begged your mother to take her to a beauty salon to fix it. She was so worried you'd hate it."

Aaron snapped on Kitty's leash and turned to Robin. "Ready?"

"Where are we going?" Robin asked.

"Downtown. Mom, Dad, and Sophie are already there. Everybody is."

Robin stepped outside and basked in the familiar damp humidity of home. The fading blue North Carolina sky was dotted with tiny wisps of clouds and the setting sun scorched the barest hint of pink on the horizon. Stately old Union Street was alive with activity. Whole families were pushing baby strollers and toting coolers downtown under the gas streetlamps of her historic neighborhood.

When Robin heard a riffing guitar and a rattle of drums, she picked up her pace, guessing what night of the month it was. She made her way past the many shoppers hustling into boutiques before they closed, and past the shuffling line waiting to buy cones at The Creamery. Up the block, she could see the police cars and barricades that blocked traffic, as the cover band swelled to a finale.

A familiar metallic voice stopped her in her tracks. "Hey, Robin," Jasmine said as she strode over. "You're not going to Union Street Live, are you?" She snorted. "Everyone over there is, like, a hundred. Including the band. I only go to see concerts in Charlotte these days, thankyouverymuch."

Robin was momentarily cowed, her mind automatically plotting excuses for why she'd want to be at such a dorky event. But on the other hand, what did

Jasmine know? Robin turned her gaze on the crowd. "Okaaay," she responded slowly. "So, how come you're here, then?"

Jasmine fumbled, clearly not expecting the question and Robin relented. "Hey, isn't that Jason over there?" She pointed in the direction of the concert.

This time Jasmine answered a little too quickly. "Oh, dunno. I broke up with him last week. See you around, Robin," and she moved quickly down the street, in the opposite direction from Jason.

In front of the grand portico of the majestic old courthouse, Union Street Live was in full gear. The event was the mayor's invention: an open-air concert that featured one local band on the third Tuesday of every summer month. Robin had always loved the event, but this summer she'd deliberately missed the first two, to stave off teasing from people like Jasmine. *Not anymore,* she thought.

As Robin caught her first glimpse of the erected stage, the dance floor, and the folding chairs that littered the lawn, a smile came to her face. Elderly Mrs. Fulghum, who lived across the street, waved while she was miming a complicated series of hand gestures and mouthing the lyrics to the Georgia Satellites song "Keep Your Hands to Yourself."

On the dance floor, next-door neighbor Miss Nancy and the other seventy-year-old line dancers turned in unison, while on the perimeter Mr. Odell shifted his hips in time with the music, careful not to put too much pressure on his prosthetic foot. Eastcliff's eight-and-under girls swim team clung to the edge of the stage, slapping high fives with the paunchy-and-balding lead singer. Robin caught sight of a white-blonde head among them, and screeched out, "SOPHIE!"

Sophie scrunched up her face in confusion as Robin came barreling toward her. Robin threw her arms around her little sister and kissed her forehead. "I've missed you so much!"

Sophie squirmed and in her most matter-of-fact voice asked, "Why are you so huggy today, Robin?" Robin's brow furrowed, then she realized Neera must've said good-bye. "I've only been down here, like . . ." Sophie scrunched up her face again, trying to calculate time. "Like an *hour*," she said finally, proud of her math.

Robin grinned at her. "Yeah? Well, it feels like longer." She craned her neck, looking over the crowd. "Where are Mom and Dad?"

Sophie pointed to the portico. "Mommy's dancing. Up there."

Robin turned to head for the portico, but stopped. "Hey, Soph? Wanna have a sleepover in my room tonight?"

Sophie had to have a think, but she finally nodded and insisted, "Okay, but I get to pick which dollies are coming!"

Robin beamed. "You're on," she said as she headed in the direction Sophie had pointed.

A couple of moms were laughingly "driving the bus" in the portico, high above the dance floor, bathed in sticky sunlight. One of them was Robin's mom. Normally, Robin would've begged her mom to stop, worried her friends might see. Tonight, she wanted to join in.

Robin wriggled her way through the crowd and took the steps two at a time, prepared to throw herself into the fray. But the band switched to a slow song, and Robin arrived just in time to see her dad catch her mom's hand and pull her in tight for a dance. She leaned against a column and watched, admiring how her mom's eyes never looked away from her dad's.

A voice snuck up behind her. "Uh, hey, Robin."

Robin turned and looked at the boy, her brain momentarily blank. She wanted to say Rupert, but she knew that was wrong. Duh! Two weeks ago this boy had been so important. As in IMPORTANT. And he'd dumped her without a word. Now he was What's-His-Name. Funny.

She grinned at him, empowered. "Hey, Jason."

Jason shuffled and looked away. "I, uh, like your hair."

"Thanks," she responded indifferently.

"Want to dance?"

Robin smiled and said, "No thanks, I'm here with my parents. It's kind of family time, ya know?" She craned her neck and pointed toward downtown. "But Jasmine's over there. I bet she'd love to dance!"

Jason suddenly seemed in a hurry. "Oh. I kinda broke up with her. Well, I'll see ya around."

"Bye." Robin shook her head as the song ended. Her mom spotted her and smiled. "You came! I'm so glad!"

Robin walked over and hugged her mom and then her dad extra hard without a word, unable to explain to them, unable to fathom how she could've ever wished herself away from such magnificently ordinary and loving parents. She finally managed a muffled, "Me too," and subtly wiped away a tear of happiness on her dad's shirt.

Her dad patted her shoulder and released her. "Hey, we were just about to gather up Sophie and get some ice cream. You want some?" His face crinkled. "Or maybe not, 'cause you're um—"

Robin interrupted him, confused. "I'm what?" Then she remembered Neera had been really grossed out by a hamburger. Maybe she didn't drink milk, either. "Never mind. I do want ice cream! It's hot! Bubblegum flavor!"

Her dad made an exaggerated gesture of wiping his forehead. "Phew! That's a relief, because for the last two weeks, your eating habits have been really, really weird!"

Aaron wanted to walk Alia home, but the rest of the Haggersly family strolled leisurely along North Union Street, devouring their cones before they melted. As they passed by the community theater, Robin noticed a new notice on the lighted marquee: AUDITIONS! *YES, VIRGINIA, THERE IS A SANTA CLAUS*, SEPTEMBER 14 & 15.

Robin turned to her mother. "What's *Yes, Virginia* about?"

Her mom looked surprised. "Huh?" She followed Robin's nod toward the marquee. "Oh. Well, let's see. It's based on a true story. A girl—I think she was about your age—wrote a letter to the newspaper, asking them whether or not Santa Claus is real. They made a movie of it, too."

Robin thought for a moment. "What did Virginia look like?"

Her mom thought for a moment and shook her head. "I don't really remember, do you, honey?" She turned to Robin's dad.

He thought. "Well, the way I remember it, she was short and had big, soulful brown eyes." He grinned at Robin. "Can't think of anybody who looks like that around here." Robin nudged him playfully, and he continued, "Why? Are you interested?"

"Yes," Robin said simply. "I'd like to try out."

Her mom raised her eyebrows. "You sure? A play is a very big commitment, Robin. If you got cast, it would mean soccer is out. Plus, it's very competitive."

Robin nodded and said, "I know. I've got a friend. A uh, pen pal actually, in England. She's only sixteen and she's a professional actress." She turned her plea on her dad. "I'd just like to try it. See if I'm any good."

Her parents communicated via a series of looks, before her dad said finally, "Well then, let's put it on the calendar and I'll bring you back for the auditions."

Robin beamed. "Cool!"

Her dad responded by lifting his arms in a cheer. "Beast!" Robin giggled, and he looked worried. "Did I do it wrong again?"

"No, you, uh, just dropped your ice cream."

He dolefully checked his empty cone and then the ground, where his rocky road was melting on the sidewalk. "Shoot."

Robin cuddled up with Sophie that night. She'd forgotten just how uncomfortable a bed full of dolls really was, but she didn't care. She was in her own room, and her little sister breathed evenly and softly in her sleep beside her.

Too excited to sleep herself, Robin was planning her copy of Fiona's famous border. Tomorrow, she'd start gathering photos.

The *matryoshkas* sat on the mantelpiece, neatly

laid out in descending order. Her mom must've put them up there while she was away. The dolls made her think of the Wishers—dolls that tucked inside other dolls, just like she'd been tucked inside Fiona's body. Robin couldn't stop staring at them. She finally realized why—an envelope was tucked in between the two biggest dolls.

Robin climbed slowly out of bed, not wanting to wake Sophie, reached up, plucked the envelope, and tiptoed into the bathroom. She switched on the light.

> *Dear Robin,*
>
> *Welcome Home! Thought of something after we talked—if you find this note right away, try to be online between seven and eight o'clock Wednesday morning your time—I think I might be able to use my teacher's computer for a few minutes.*
>
> *I will miss you. Good luck to both of us tonight!*
>
> *Love,*
> *Neera*

Something nagged at Robin's brain, but she was suddenly too tired to remember what it was. She yawned heavily, hoping she'd remember when she talked to Neera in the morning. She went back to her bedroom and set the alarm for six o'clock, determined not to miss her.

I just can't believe it's over!!! I'm so happy!!!

Robin thrilled at Fiona's post, but she was somewhat impatient to hear from Neera. She'd been sitting at the computer for more than an hour in her bathrobe. She'd even double-checked the time difference between North Carolina and India: seven in the morning here was four thirty in the evening there.

A chat room popped up in the corner of Robin's screen and her hopes rose. But it was Fiona.

OMG! Robin! Thank you!!!!!!!!!!!!!!!!!!!!!!!!!!!!!!!!!

A moment later, Fiona typed again.

I don't even mind that you got to meet Prince William.

Robin finally typed back.

WELL, AT LEAST YOU GET TO ENJOY ALL THE ATTENTION FROM IT. HOW'S THE PHOTO?

Brill! Front page of The Guardian. Will send u link. U have to see Jo's review, 2. Oh, & Headmaster called. I'm reinstated and get to re-sit Eleven Plus!!!

THAT'S GREAT, FIONA.

What did you say to Rupert, BTW? He ducked me on the street.

I CALLED HIM A BIG GIRL'S BLOUSE.

rofl!!!

IS JOLENE THERE WITH YOU?

Nah. She wouldn't let me out of her sight last night, but RADA called & said she had 2 sign paperwork today or give up her spot.

SHE GOT IN? THAT'S AWESOME!

We're all going out tonight to celebrate. It's nice, u know, 2 feel genuinely happy 4 my sister. How's things your end?

GREAT. SO GOOD TO SEE MY FAMILY AGAIN. JUST WISH—OOPS, NOT THAT WORD—WOULD LIKE TO HEAR FROM NEERA.

I'm sure she's great.

On instinct, Robin decided to ask Fiona about the timing of the wish.

HEY, FIONA, WHAT TIME DID YOU WISH?

??? 10 p.m. London time. Like u said.

NO ONE TOLD YOU TO WISH AT 9:45?

No. Hey, gotta go, Mum's calling. B 4 N.

Now Robin was confused. The wish had been moved, hadn't it? To 9:45? She'd wished at 9:45 and she was home. Naomi was home. Fiona was home. Neera HAD to be home. She was the only other girl wishing!

But how could that be, if they didn't wish all at the same time?

Uncomfortable, Robin darted into the kitchen and asked her mom, "Is Aaron awake?"

"Awake and already gone, mowing lawns. He won't be back for hours. Have some breakfast, sweetie."

Robin shook her head. "I'm not hungry. Uh, is Alia coming over?"

Her mom looked at her and sighed. "Robin, I'm glad you like Alia, and I appreciate that she's your friend, too, but I told you at the beach that you need to give Aaron and Alia a little space. You said you would, but then you came right back and spent the entire day with both of them."

Robin started to protest, but she realized Neera must've been spending loads of time with Alia while trying to find all the Wishers. Since none of her family knew about wishing, they must've thought she was trying to hog Aaron's girlfriend. She wondered how that must've felt for Aaron.

Her mom continued, "How about you call Wrenn today instead?"

Robin nodded and returned to the computer. There was nothing to do but wait in hope that Neera would contact her.

Half an hour later, the chat room popped up again.

I'm home!!!!!!!!!!!!!!!! Sorry I'm late. My teacher wasn't home. Had 2 wait.

Robin typed furiously.

NEERA! OMG! UR OK! I WAS SO WORRIED!

Yeah, all that stuff with Dori was a little scary.

WHAT STUFF WITH DORI?

Neera's pause was incredibly long. So long that Robin was forced to prompt her again.

Y S T?

Yeah.

NEERA, WHAT HAPPENED? I GOT A TEXT FROM DORI, TELLING ME TO WISH AT 9:45. I WISHED AND YOU MUST'VE WISHED. BUT FIONA AND NAOMI WISHED AT 10. BUT WE'RE ALL HOME. ALIA WAS TRYING 2 TELL ME SOMETHING WAS WEIRD, BUT SHE SAID WE HAD 2 WAIT AND TALK 2 U.

Dori lied about the wish time. It was always set for 10 pm London, 5 in NC. We found out she lied 2 u, but 2 late 2 contact u.

WHY WOULD DORI DO THAT?

So u would wish, & she would wish. Just the 2 of u. & then she'd be Fiona.

Robin was thunderstruck.

WHY????

She thought she'd be a big star in London. Something about the Jonas Bros?

Jolene's lies! Robin had known they were a mistake. But she never dreamed Dori would be so mean. That Dori would be willing to trick her! And what about Naomi? And Neera? They could've been stuck forever! As in, FOREVER. Aaron's words came ringing back in Robin's ears: *While you're eyeing someone else's stuff, somebody's eyeing yours.* Now she understood what that meant.

I THOUGHT SHE WANTED 2 BE SAMANTHA FOREVER.

I know. But I guess she changed her mind.

Whatever magic was working this, Robin decided, was absolutely nuts. Because any eleven-year-old girl would always find fault with herself, every time. And that same eleven-year-old girl would also find perfection in some other girl and wish she was that girl. But no amount of wishing yourself into someone else's life and body would make it better. You'd just keep finding fault with who you were, and somebody else's life would still look better than yours. There was no magic in being somebody else—the true magic was in discovering who you already *are*. It had taken Robin becoming Fiona Walker to learn that Robin Haggersly was talented and smart and maybe even a little pretty. Even if she was short.

Robin finally typed back.

HOW DID U FIND OUT?

Samantha De Groot.

HUH???!!!!

Remember how Dori gave us Samantha's email? & Alia got really suspicious?

SO???

Well, Alia called Dori's house in Hawaii. Just 2 find out who Dori's wisher was. It was Samantha! They were a straight switch! & Dori had been refusing 2 wish back, for, like, months. She wouldn't even return Samantha's calls.

WHOA.

I know, right??? Anyway, Alia got Samantha 2 talk. Samantha admitted she sent u that mean email because she looked at our FB page. She saw Dori listed as a friend & thought we all had to be like Dori.

AS IN, WISHERS WHO DON'T WANT 2 GO HOME.

Exactly. Anyway, Alia convinced her we weren't. Told her how we were planning 2 wish. Samantha freaked out. Dori had suddenly called her & told her she could "have her stupid body back" if she wished at 9:45 London time. Dori bragged she was going 2 be a big star. Then we knew what Dori was up to. But it was 2 late 2 call u. U were at the theater.

SO WHAT DID U DO? HOW COME I'M HOME?

Samantha & I wished. We agreed we'd wish at 9:45, so Dori would have less chance of becoming Fiona & mess everything up.

SO, WAIT, WHAT HAPPENED?

I became Fiona for, like, 15 minutes. So glad u were sitting down in that theater & had cell phone in ur hand!!! I was so dizzy & i had to keep an eye on the time. Had to wish again at 10!

U WISHED TWICE???!!!! IN FIFTEEN MINUTES??

Y. Samantha and I both did. She insisted if Dori failed at 9:45, she'd try again at 10. So provided we didn't end up in our own bodies with first wish, we'd try again at 10 with everybody else.

Now Robin was confused.

WHAT???

Here's Sam's thinking: Dori's trying to wish just with Fiona. So we go the other way—everybody wish. Include Dori and Sam. See? Then everybody wishing has a good chance of going home. Cause we're all in each other's bodies. Anyway, it worked. I'm home.

Robin was overwhelmed.

BUT NEERA, WHY WOULD U DO THAT?

Because u could've gone home the very first day. U stayed in England 4 me. I owed u.

U DID NOT—

Neera interrupted her.

Listen. It worked. Ur home, I'm home.

Robin hesitated but finally asked.

DO U THINK DORI AND SAMANTHA ARE HOME, 2?

Probably. Hey, I have 2 go.

NO! WAIT! I STILL HAVE QUESTIONS!!!

Teacher says I have 2 go. No choice.

OKAY, BUT PROMISE U'LL STAY IN TOUCH? NEERA, NO ONE'S EVER DONE ANYTHING 4 ME LIKE WHAT U DID. UR AS MUCH MY BFF AS WRENN IS.

U 2. B 4 N.

Robin's mom popped her head through the library door. "Again? I'm going to deactivate that Facebook page unless you get dressed. C'mon, right now, missy."

"Where are we going?" Robin asked.

"School shopping, of course! Told you yesterday. All the big sales are on."

School? Again? Robin mentally counted the days

to her own school opening. Yeah, it was time to go shopping. Plus, this wasn't any old school shopping trip—she was going to middle school!

She wiggled with excitement and then laughed. It was okay to wiggle! She was Robin Haggersly again!

Robin thought about her grandmother's birthday message—eleven is a magical number. Her grandmother was right. So far, being eleven was absolutely amazing. She'd been a Wisher, a magic few people knew existed and even fewer people got a chance to try. She'd traveled abroad—to England! And actually lived there! She'd performed in a professional play. As the star! And she'd discovered she was pretty good at it! Then she'd wished again, like the heroine in a movie, and gotten herself, Neera, Naomi, and Fiona—girls from every corner of the globe—home. Now she was about to start middle school. She couldn't wait.

Being an eleven-year-old isn't just magical, Robin realized. It's as exciting as standing onstage, watching the curtain go up. Because everything changed when she turned eleven—her body, her thinking, even who she was, where she was, and what she did every day. And she was sure there were more changes coming. She could feel it like an electrical current, whizzing through her body. And even though she'd make more mistakes, or maybe sometimes she might look or feel a little weird, the biggest truth she needed to remember was she'd change again before long. That's just what eleven-year-olds do.

There was absolutely no chance—no matter how bad things got—that she'd ever wish again. Sure, there were going to be girls who were maybe prettier, more popular, smarter, or more talented than herself, and sometimes their lives might look better than her own. But they weren't. In fact, chances were that girl, whoever she might be, would be comparing herself unfavorably to somebody else at the same time.

To be successful at being eleven years old, Robin decided, you had to look forward to each change in who you are, where you are, or what you look like. You had to think of each and every one as a new adventure. Because some of those changes are going to be pretty good. And some will even be great.

epilogue

Dori Simpson of Honolulu, Hawaii

NEERA HAD LIED. SHE DIDN'T LIKE LYING and she rarely did, but this time it was necessary, because she didn't want to ruin Robin's happiness. She'd meant what she'd said: Robin was her BFF. Robin had made an enormous sacrifice for her by staying in England for two and a half weeks, when she could've wished, gone home, and left Neera to her problems as a Wisher. But Robin didn't do that. She'd stayed Fiona, as long as it took to find Neera's Wisher, and she'd done so without hesitation. Robin's self-sacrifice deserved an equal measure of self-sacrifice

Neera had been so angry as when she'd found out what Dori planned to do, that Dori intended to trick Robin into wishing at 9:45. She'd tried to stop Dori—she was hugely frustrated when she couldn't get in touch with Robin on Tuesday night before the wish. When that failed, all Neera could do was join the 9:45 wish, hoping against hope that Robin would get home. And Robin had gone home.

A small surge of triumph ignited inside her once again. Worth it. Her sacrifice was worth it. Robin was home, and so were Naomi and Fiona. Okay, she'd had the teensiest hope when she wished again at 10:00 that she'd get home to India, but she'd guessed that was probably asking too much of the magic.

Neera switched off Dori's laptop, hit the light, and pulled Dori's fuzzy pink quilt over herself in the bed. She'd wished twice in the last twenty-four hours and been forced to stay up really, really late, just so she could pretend she was home in India. She was absolutely exhausted. She'd worry about where Dori and Samantha were tomorrow. Maybe she'd even tell Robin the truth at some point. Or maybe, at some point soon, Dori would want to wish herself home to Hawaii, and Neera's lie wouldn't matter.

It could happen. You never know with Wishers.